# DEAR MONSTER CLAUS

## MAEVE BLACK

© 2022 Maeve Black

All Rights Reserved

Editor & Proof: Rumi Khan

Illustrator: Vamorii

Cover: www.opulentswaganddesigns.com

No part of this book may be reproduced, copied or transmitted in any form or by any means, electronic or mechanical, including photocopying, recording, or by any information storage or retrieval system without written expressed permission from the author, except in the case of brief quotations embodied in critical articles or reviews.

This book is intended for adults who are of eighteen years of age, or older.

This is a work of fiction. Names, characters, businesses, places, events, and incidents are products of the author's imagination and are used fictitiously. Any resemblance to actual persons, living or dead, events or locales is purely coincidental.

This book is licensed for your personal enjoyment. This book may not be re-sold or given away to other people. If you would like to share this book with another person, please purchase an additional copy for each recipient. If you are reading this book and did not purchase it, or if it was not purchased for your use only, then you should return it to the seller and please purchase your own copy.

All rights reserved. Except as permitted under the U.S. Copyright act of 1976, no part of this publication may be reproduced, distributed, or transmitted in any form or by any means, or stored in a database or retrieval system, without the prior express, written consent of the author.

# DEAR MONSTER CLAUS

## MAEVE BLACK

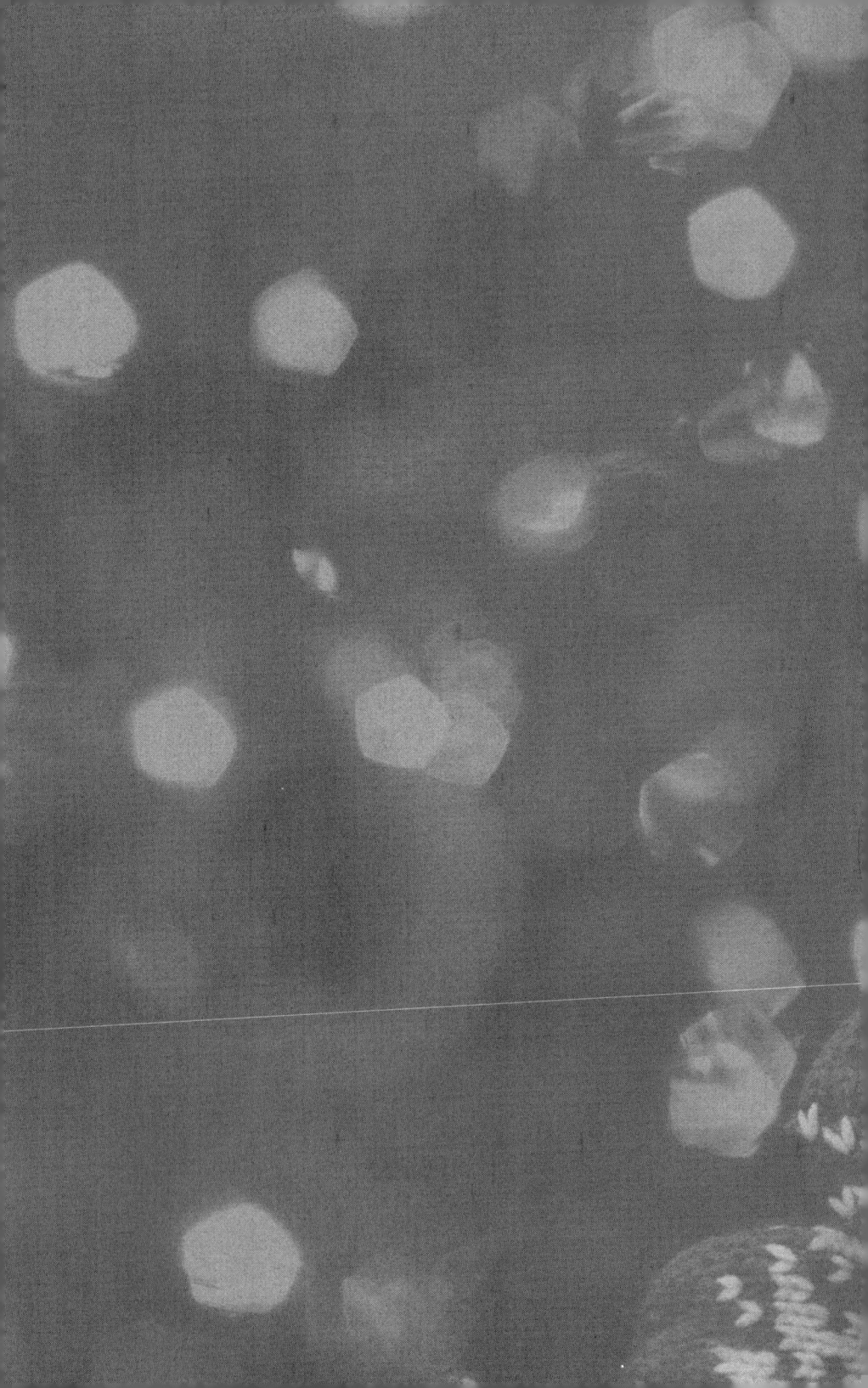

## PEPPERMINT WHITE RUSSIAN

Drink responsibly and only if you're of legal drinking age.

4oz Kahlua Coffee Liquor
2oz Peppermint Schnapps or Peppermint Vodka
1oz Bailey's Liquor (your choice of flavoring)
Add your choice of milk additive. Whether that be almond, coconut, oat, soy, etc. It's based on preference on how much but I like equal parts of my Kahlua.
Top over ice, add whip cream up top and peppermint sprinkles as a garnish.

## XO'S VIRGIN PEPPERMINT COFFEE

8oz of a light roast coffee. If you want cold brew, do 12oz.
*If you do cold brew, add everything over ice.*
2oz of your choice of milk additive. I prefer heavy whipping cream
1tbsp of peppermint syrup (More if you're wanting a stronger flavor)
1 tbsp of Ghirardelli White Mocha syrup
*Make sure you warm up your milk additive and froth it. The frothing isn't necessary but the warming is. You can add the flavor syrups to the milk additive too. Unless you went with cold brew. If you did, nix the heating portion.*
Top with whipping cream and peppermint sprinkles.
(I just add crushed candy cane dust)

# Content Warnings

They are detailed on this page so please skip if you don't want spoiler-y stuff.

# Last Chance...

If you don't like pregnancy trope, don't read the second epilogue.

There are sexual situations with teaching sex acts, honorifics, squirting, anal, praise, breeding kink, shibari-lite with ribbon, peppermint cum, a candy cane dick, a sex swing, drool-play, salirophilia, (he really likes making her messy with his release.) There's virgin sex without condoms. There is what's called the *melt*, which is their equivalent to omega/alpha traits.

'Twas the night
before Christmas
when all through the house
all creatures were stirring
*especially* a mouse—I mean, Cupid.

To everyone who always wondered
what it would be like to be
dicked down with a candy cane.

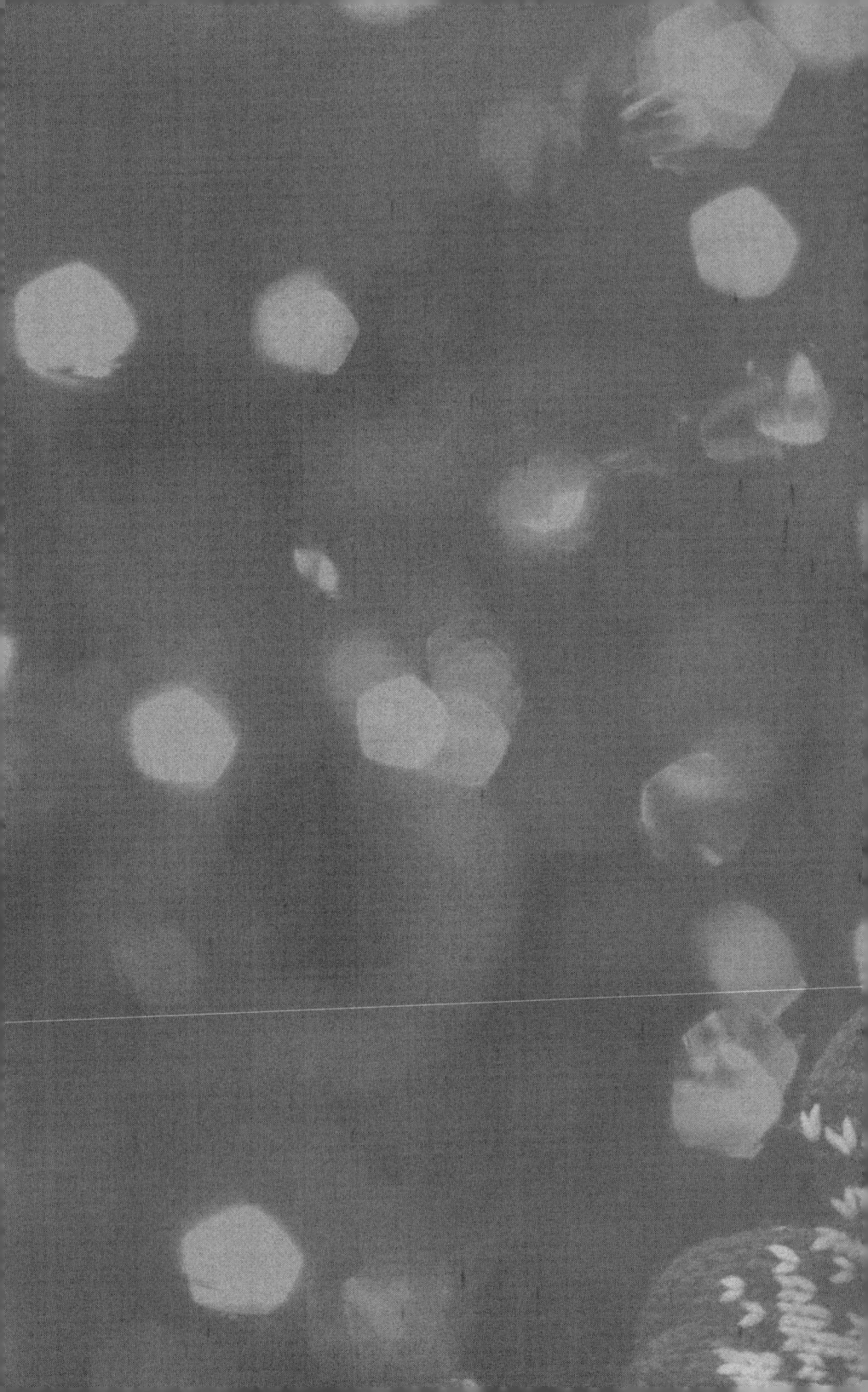

# CHAPTER 1

### JINGLE BELL ROCK — BOBBY HELMS

### XO

Another romance in the books, and once again, it's not mine.

The couple in question was two women. Fiona and Lena. When given their names on the *lucky-in-love* list, excitement filled me. They'd never met, the tension had my palms sweating with nerves. It can go so many ways, but theirs painted a softer and new picture. Two women who hid for so long and finally found each other in the end. As soon as I passed them both, I sent them silent love magic.

They'd get married, grow a life together, and create a little antique shop in town. One I'll be back to visit in a few years.

Now, I sit in the tiny coffee shop at the edge of Mistletoe Grove, drinking away my hopes and desires for my own future.

My sisters, Dulce and Dionysius, chat with other humans, pushing them toward their soul mates while I stand near Valentine. Unlike the three of us, he doesn't have a charge. He's just not too fond of being around our parents.

Instead, we drag him around with us during his downtime.

He's downing some Christmas concoction I convinced him to try, his face scrunched with displeasure. "How do you drink this shit?" I lift my mug, the reindeer with a red nose on the ceramic smiling back at me. I haven't tried this year's recipe, but last year's was hazelnut and toffee surprise.

Taking a sip, warmth fills my body. Flavors coat my tongue, tasting like holiday spirit. Cinnamon, chocolate, and a bit of clove. Steam rises from the cup, making little swirls as my brother dramatically rolls his eyes. His fingers tap on his backup cup of Earl Grey.

"It tastes like Christmas in a cup," I persist, smacking my lips to figure out the last flavor that evades me. *Maybe it's nutmeg?*

Val narrows his eyes at me and then my drink as if it offends him. His lips form around the edge of the cup as he tastes it once more.

"Christmas in a cup? More like I'm licking a pine tree in the dead of winter," he grumbles, gagging openly.

I laugh at his annoyance, patting his shoulder. He was never one for festivity or the cold. I nod toward our sisters, wondering how they commit to giving everyone love without questioning where our happy endings lie.

We could find love for any person in all the realms, yet we don't get it ourselves? Make it make sense. I've felt like such an outsider in my realm and family. I'm the only one hoping what only mortals wish for.

It's ridiculous, knowing that my people judge me for having ideas of happiness.

I want a man, but not any man. I want one who wants me and *only me*.

"Why don't we get to have love?" I gently whisper, hoping *he* didn't hear. It's a topic of contention between us. Hades, I even know his response—he gives it often. He's always telling me to stop being so obsessed with the idea of romance. It's not for *us*.

We have rules.

Drinking more, I eye him and note his wrung-out expression. His eyebrows draw inward, pinching while his lips purse, yet he says nothing. A tic in his jaw forms too, it's his usual bitter expression. A mix of disappointment and annoyance.

We're Cupids, the myths, or rather the reality. There isn't just one of us, it's a family business. We all play our parts, helping the world find their forever partners.

"Xóchitl," he sighs with exasperation. Val only uses my full name when he isn't happy. Usually, it's Xó or Xóchi. With a shake of his head, he pats my arm. "We're not meant to find what we give others. That's what makes us perfect for the job. We don't seek that kind of thing. We're not created to."

Yet, my yearning lingers, growing stronger with every passing match. Why not us? We don't even experience love through our charges. It's like we witness it, seeing it through their eyes, without ever knowing the feeling.

"Why though? Why can't I experience hugs, kisses, and possibly more?"

He cringes, almost like I'm reading my diary out loud. "That's just not in the cards for us."

Anger rises in me. None of my siblings seem to care, but every time I see someone fall in love, watch their eyes shine with hope and infatuation, I sadden further. I've never felt it, I've never experienced warmth in that way, I've never had sex, or even had an orgasm. I've never even *kissed* someone before.

My cheeks warm, thinking of how embarrassing it must be to others to know I'm as old as I am and have never experienced affection.

"I want to experience love," I solemnly admit, my voice quieting. Gripping my mug like it's a protectant, I wait for his reactionary response. It's still warm, but the cold bitterness inside me festers at the possibility that I'll never truly be happy. "I want to experience romance."

I can only talk to Val. Dion and Dulce make fun of my desire for simple things. They're twins and don't understand humanity or its need for emotions. That's probably why they toy with them so much.

Val shakes his head again, his jaw clenched. He's probably sick of my wondrous questions, but until there's a definitive answer other than *just because*, I'll continue to question everything. My brother and I are closest. Not only in age, but in similarities. We have the same hobbies and joys. Except that he hates Christmas—and holidays altogether. Whereas I could live every single day as a holiday and never grow tired.

"Can't you distract yourself?" he grumpily wonders. "It's Christmas, you like Christmas. Maybe it'll get your mind off what's off-limits for us."

My lip protrudes as I acknowledge my true denial. I've helped thousands find love. Why is it so hard for me?

We're taught young; Cupids don't find love, they give it. They don't find contentment, they let others experience it. They don't get romance, they simply thrust it upon others.

I've never wanted to deny my heritage or family business more than now. I stare at the surrounding shops. The dangling lights, window-painted snowmen, and how there's a massive tree in the center of town, illuminating everything. Or it will be once Christmas week hits.

Mistletoe Grove is where we go every year. They gave each Cupid family an area. We're fortunate to go to the human realm, to a place where they celebrate holidays.

Back in Darchon, we don't have such celebrations. It's gloomy all year, wars are always on the cusp. But here exists joy, laughter, cookies, and love. Val stares at me, his eyes almost studying as I absorb the merriment of the town.

"Fine, but don't harass me when I end up staying here for the winter," I nonchalantly shrug, taking another drink, and decide that's what I'll do. There are no other love matches on my duties until New Year's. All I have is time.

Val offers a small smile. He doesn't like when I'm sad. Unlike him and our sisters, I'm the youngest. They say that's why I always crave forbidden things, but I wonder if they're just lost.

"If you stay too long, we'll have to come back and drag you home. Especially if you miss a check-in. We all know you hate writing letters." He says this with raised eyebrows and a spark of amusement. He may be jaded from the Cupid business, but he's always been an amazing brother.

"Thanks, Val." I push out my chair, reaching for him to hug. He gives me an awkward side one. Another thing we don't do. *Affection.* Cupids call hugs human behavior. He's wrong. Even when we're in Darchon, giving love magic to monsters and fae alike, we see them embrace.

"Now, go." He shoos me, his hands waving quickly. "Dion and Dulce won't like you going off."

"That's because they're boring workaholics with no hobbies," I mutter grumpily, thinking of how they always tease me for my fascinations. Humor lights his features, his dimples peeking through.

"They like teasing poor human boys," he argues, but he's very amused.

"That's not a hobby, Val," I grumble, thinking about how they can turn invisible and cause chaos. "That's called harassment."

I set down my nearly empty mug and grab my bag with our special letters that'll send directly to my home in Darchon. Cupids are magical, not like wizards or Wiccans, but definitely in their own right. We could create love, manipulate the weather, and induce happiness temporarily.

"See you after Christmas!" I call out, heading toward the door before he can argue. Sometimes, while Val tries his best, he still dampers my mood. He's moody and unhappy.

Now it's time to find love. No matter how asinine it sounds to everyone else. Val might think I'm celebrating Christmas—which I will—but my intentions are clear. I'll find my happy ending this December.

# CHAPTER 2

## A HOLLY JOLLY CHRISTMAS — BURL IVES

## XO

**C**old welcomes me back at the cabin. It sits at the opposite edge of town. Old, but furnished, and so stunning during the winter. I've been here for over a week, and already I'm settled in comfortably.

We've had this place for generations. A home to escape to if we're stuck in the snow for the winter. Mistletoe Grove gets blizzards that are insanely packed. Where you can't even make it to a portal and head home.

I need to go into town for snacks. Not because I need human food to sustain me, but because it's my guilty pleasure. Especially sweets. Candy canes, cookies, and gingerbread. My absolute weaknesses.

Pulling on my dress, I go for simple. An ugly green sweater dress with little reindeer on them. It's so contrasting against my skin that it'll possibly act as a distraction.

I'm a pink color, more like light bubble gum rather than bright pink.

All Cupids have different pigmentation. Val is redder in tone, while Dion is lavender and Dulce is a peach. I think it's the only way they tell us apart.

We're similar in the looks department, especially since Dion and Dulce are twins. Our noses match and our lips too. Our eyes all match our skin tones, unironically. If not for cosplayers in the human realm, our coloring would stand out more, be awkward even. We get comments, but using the 'oh, we're from a convention' has them moving along.

Unlike many faefolk from Darchon, we don't have any fun attributes other than our coloring. If dragons were still around, they'd have scales and wings. Of course, they can glamour those, but they generally showed them. Even many incubi have horns and tails, and then there are the *Saephyn*. They have *fangs!* They don't like being called vamps, though.

After putting on some makeup, I head for the mall in town. There's only one, plus many mom-and-pop shops that have gifts and more niche items.

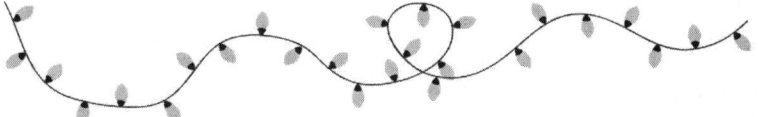

Once I arrive, I note all the Christmas lights twinkling. It's always so bright here, everyone's so nice and cheery. It's as if they save all the kindness for the month of December.

They decorated the inside with so many icicles, cut-out snowflakes, inflated snowmen, and even a Grinch holding a wreath mischievously. People mill about paying no mind to the beauty that is this place, but I stop at every shop to gawk.

Little kids giggle and one says, "Santa is here. He's granting wishes."

I'm not naïve, I've been told Santa is fictional. Something big businesses created to garner more money. But what if he's not? What if, like Cupids, he's very much *real*? I've watched movies, they're so cheerful and cute, and Santa always grants the good kids happiness. My heart races at the possibility, the acknowledgment that he could grant me my one wish.

*Love.*

Most people wish for money, success, or even something big. I just want to find love.

"Think he'll get me a guitar?" one kid asks, taking a bite out of a soft pretzel. Their face is full of excitement, something I feel reflected in me.

"Didn't you kick Mr. Daniel's a couple months ago?" another child asks with a raised eyebrow. They drink something and silently judge their friend.

"Yeah, but I apologized!" the first kid shouts, their face wobbling with worry. I know that if I made a single mistake and lost all chances at love, I'd be near tears too.

"Don't be mean, Rach. Johnny didn't mean it. Santa is forgiving," one parries, wrapping their arm around the one they called Johnny. I want to hug them both, tell them their hearts are big and compassion is such a wonderful trait, but I don't. Instead, they trail off and I look for this Santa fellow.

While meandering, the scent of cinnamon and cardamom distracts me. My nose drags me to a little shop, filled with nuts, roasted and coated ones specifically. A petite older person in a dress stands at the counter, cheeks red and sporting the cutest gray curls.

"Hello, dear," they offer, their voice cheery and kind.

"It smells delicious," I muse, taking in a deep breath and laughing when the person scrunches their face in amusement.

"They're quite tasty. I definitely recommend the pecans," they suggest, walking toward a tower of bags. The cellophane is decorated with tiny trees and stars. "It's the perfect mixture of sweet and salty."

"I'll take one!" My mind fills with the desire to munch them all down. The clerk ties off a bag with some frilly metallic material and heads to the register. I realize there's a chance that they know where Santa is. "Do you know where Santa is?" I shyly ask, not wanting to get a weird look from the person.

"Oh, yes! He's in the center of the mall. You won't miss the North Pole. There are lights and a Candy Cane Lane." They pause, smiling widely. "There are reindeer and a huge throne, too."

"How does one ask for a wish?" I awkwardly ask, hope sliding through me like the best tasting hot cocoa.

"You sit on his lap and ask for what you want. Be specific and try to ask for only one thing," they offer with a nod. Handing over my nuts, they point toward what I'm guessing is the center of the mall. "Head that way. You can't miss it. And if he doesn't respond the way you want, you can always mail Santa a letter. Those, he always reads thoroughly."

"Thank you so much!" The way hope soaks me with happiness has me skipping in the direction they told me to go.

MAEVE BLACK

# CHAPTER 3

## SANTA CLAUS IS COMING TO TOWN — THE JACKSON 5

## XO

They weren't joking.

There are lights *everywhere*. Leading to the big chair in the center are candy canes, little lollies, and so many piles of fake snow.

Kids are dancing and giggling, and the elves they have are adorable with their little green and red stripes.

Everything is so perfect.

Exactly how movies depict it. With smiling parents, kids making wishes, and a Santa somewhere in there too.

"Do you want a photo?"

I don't notice who says it until there's a tap on my shoulder. As I turn, a grumpy-looking person's frown greets me.

"A photo?" I question, trying not to be rude.

"Listen, lady, if you won't pay, Santa won't want to see you."

Pay?

Cupids can't receive money or other gain to do our duty. We're honored to deliver with nothing as payment.

I pull out cash, offering it. "Is this—"

They grab it from my hand and nod. "All right, go on up the steps and meet him. Your photo will be available as soon as you're done."

Photo? Why would I need a photo?

I start to ask a question but they push me toward the roped-off area before I get a chance. "Hurry it up before you miss your chance."

And I thought everyone was nice during Christmas.

Unhurriedly, I stare at the decorations. This is exactly what I want at the cottage. Lights, snow, and holiday cheer. It's not too much to ask for.

"Ho, ho, ho, there!" a jolly voice shouts. It's full of depth and laced with tiredness. As soon as I climb up the last steps to the platform, I notice a man in a red suit.

It's dark crimson, almost like candy apple red and blood created a color together. His eyes are wide and questioning. It takes me a few seconds to wonder if it's my skin color.

"Are you one of my helpers?" he asks, his white beard wiggling with his words. I step toward him, getting closer to his lap.

"No, not me. Just a girl after a wish."

His face doesn't change. It's still curious and confused, all in one. "Sit on Santa's lap," he ho-hums, as if this is such a normal and boring occasion. After all, I'm no one special. Just another person asking for something.

I move until I'm hovering over his knee and lower myself. Immediately, I wonder how odd an adult woman appears sitting on his lap.

"Let me guess, you want your boyfriend to propose and get you a big fancy ring?"

I scrunch my face, thinking of how vain people can be. Sure, being engaged is so romantic, but a ring isn't what I'd wish for.

With a shake of my head, I finally respond. "Well, Santa. You see..." I pause, watching the old man's patience wear thin. "I want to find my happy ending. I want love." It's simple, straight to the point, and while he doesn't laugh at me, he gives me a raised eyebrow similar to Val's.

"Lady, I'm just a mall Santa. Are the other helpers asking you to play a joke on me? We simply don't have time for it."

My heart pounds at the implications of him thinking this is some prank. My wishes aren't so far-fetched or too unrealistic... are they?

As someone who grants love often, it's as easy as a touch or a blown kiss. It's not rocket science.

"You're telling me you can't even grant me something as simple as love?"

He loses it then, nearly knocking me off his lap. His head goes back with his exaggerated guffaw. "I'm only here to make some fast cash. Go bother someone else."

I rush to escape, my cheeks burning with embarrassment. How can he be so cruel? Maybe Santa *isn't* real.

Heading toward the stairs, I take them two at a time, retreating as quickly as I can. This is so awkward. Santa's ho, ho, ho echoes as he welcomes the next person.

A booth sits at the opposite end of the lane. A person stands there, smacking gum obnoxiously, their expression bored. "Here's your photo, ma'am."

The small picture is visible, and it shows the fake-Santa laughing and my horrified expression. How can they ask for money when this is the result?

I snatch it, nearly tripping over my feet to escape this nightmare. This can't be how it's supposed to happen.

Maybe I need a distraction.

I close my eyes, near tears, and escape the mall. Each step away, my shoulders relax. Christmas is supposed to be jubilant, full of fun and warmth.

No matter what, I'll find love. Even if their lame fake-Santa can't help me.

# CHAPTER 4

## BLUE CHRISTMAS — ELVIS PRESLEY

# ARSON

"You can't sit around all season," my brother Pyro complains as I sit at my desk. It's not even decorated this year. It's empty, along with all the joy I used to find this time of year.

"Seems like I can," I grumble, thinking about how the entire human realm depends on me. If they knew I wasn't human or a jolly old fuck, would they even be desperate for my kindness?

I didn't sign up to be a Santa. We're born into our burdens, and as the oldest, I'm required to do it until I settle down. Settling down sounds just as miserable.

Pyro glares at me as I tap my pen, not signing off the list. I'm not checking it once, nor will I be dragging myself through it twice.

There's something so exhausting about making the world happy when I can't muster a smile myself.

"Ugh," he laments, leaning on my desk. Our faces are far too close. His olive-green eyes which match mine perfectly search my face. "It's not my fault you were born first."

I throw my hands up, wanting nothing more than to hand the mantle his way. "By all means, brother. Take the fucking glory, I don't want it."

He shakes his head immediately. "That's not how it works. We're not gifted this. It's a birthright."

"Never asked for it," I complain once more under my breath. But he's not having it. His face screws up in anger and he hands me letters.

There are always so many damn letters.

"Maybe read some of these, find your holly jolly bullshit, and suck it up. Until you find a person to wed and breed with, you don't have the luxury of taking Christmas off."

"Thanks, Dad. I wasn't aware."

Heat blazes behind his eyes, reddening his navy skin. That's where we differ. My brother is a deep navy blue, and I'm more of a bloody red.

Oh, and we're dragons.

Forgot that little tidbit.

"Read these," he grouches, tapping the ones he set down. My eyes catch on a bright pink one, and for some reason, it draws me in.

I wave him off. With minor complaint, he shuffles out, leaving me with my yearly scheduled case of bah humbug.

It's not like I've hated Christmas since the beginning, but when you do it year after year, the naughty list lengthening from selfishness and anger, I tire of the same old.

My hand still grips the pink letter. It's a specific shade of pink. Like chewed bubble gum from those old quarter gumball machines.

Bringing it to my nose, I inhale and the potent scent of candy hits my nose. It's not real candy, not graspable, but what bottled sweetness smells like.

I close my nose and inhale once more, wondering why my body warms up the way it is. I'm almost always hot. Being a fire breather does that to a person, but this is a different heat.

Placing my claw beneath the tiny flap, I slide it across, noting it's also kissed. There's a pinkish press of lips on the envelope.

It's not signed on the back, or addressed to anyone. How did this person know it would get to me? Were they just betting on me receiving it?

Slipping the pink paper out, that same sugary aroma wafts in the air and I hum at the way it comforts me.

The letter has the cutest handwriting and as soon as my eyes land on the first sentence, I know I've fucked up.

---

*Dear Santa, (or is it Mr. Claus?)*

*Do you have a preference of titling? It's day four of writing you. I know this is my fourth letter and I'm sure with your lack of response, you're sick of me writing to you. Understandable, I'm sure.*

*But you see, I need to find love. I've heard you grant wishes to good girls. And believe me when I say I've been really good.*

*How can I prove it? Shall I list some deeds? Please help a girl out, Santa.*

*My heart aches to know what true love feels like and if I'm even worthy of finding it.*

*If I could make it happen myself, I would. I'm just not magical in that way.*

*With all my Christmas cheer,*
*Cupid*

I can't tell if I'm smiling with amusement or her obvious agitation with my lack of response. I'm supposed to read and respond to letters. Not all, but especially those of continuous writers. They're usually children, hoping, praying for a miracle. They want health and good fortune, but I can tell this is a grown woman. She even claims it's her fourth letter.

Intrigue to do something *different* lights a new fire inside me.

I stand at the letter bin overflowing with letters upon letters. Digging until I find similar pink ones, I fish them out. Each one smells similar, but the one that specifically smells like peppermint candy canes does something to me.

My heart hammers and my dick twitches. It's one scent that sends me down a primal spiral. I'd love to coat her in the scent and sniff her until she begs me to stop.

Shaking my head at the inappropriate thoughts, I cringe. That's unlike me and so fucking creepy. Yet, a small part of me still wants that visual to come to fruition.

> Dear Santa,
> (or Mr. Claus or man with a red getup)
>
> I'm writing you to tell you I'm desperate. It's day ten. You see, I've been trying to find love for years, and this year, I threw caution to the wind and asked a stranger. Can you grant me this one wish? I've heard you're a giving man and I'm a giving girl. We could trade? I'll do whatever you want, it's just important I find true love this year. I'm on my hands and knees, Santa.
>
> Sincerely,
> A Very Good Girl

A new sensation fills me, throbs between my legs, and overwhelms my senses. I'm sure she didn't intend to bring me that visual, but with it smelling like peppermint and her on her knees… Shit. Yeah, my face hurts from the way I'm smiling. This charismatic character has me intrigued. I shuffle through the next one, wondering what it says.

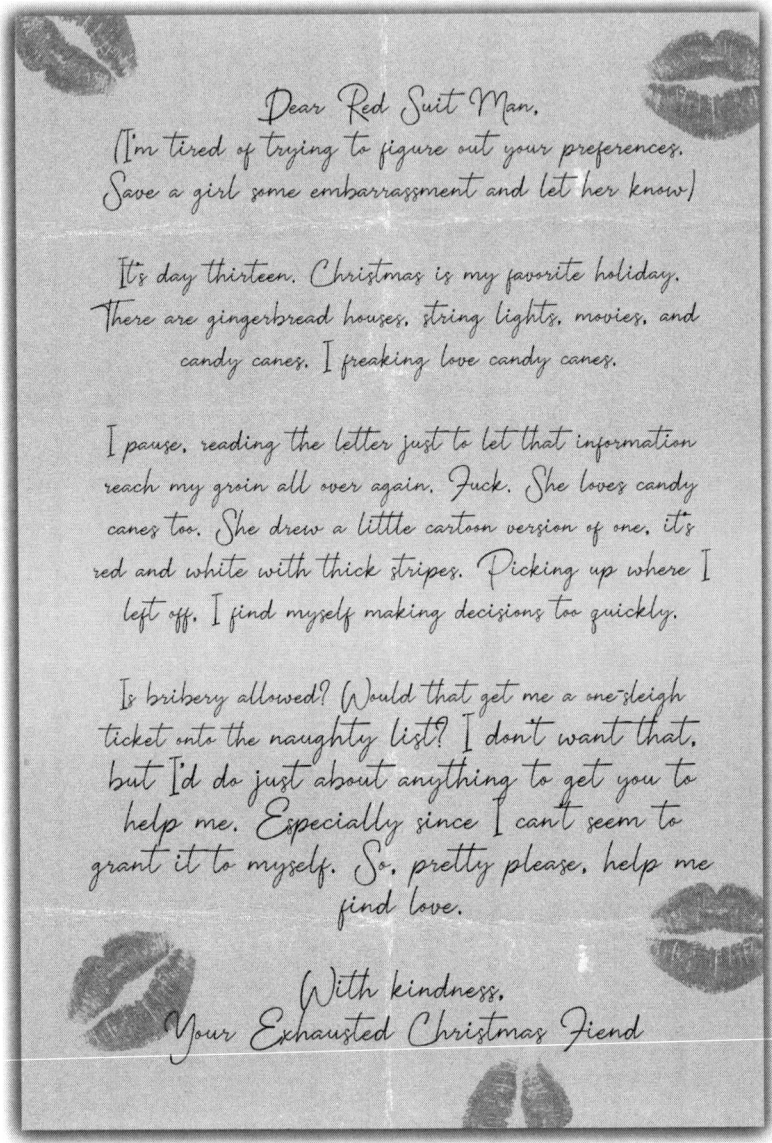

I'm practically running to my room, my feet pound far too aggressively and Pyro notices me. "What has you in a hurry?" Amusement on my brother is as grating as anger. They both seem to be present and condescending somehow.

"Mistletoe Grove."

He narrows his gaze, distrust and confusion there now. "Leaving a week before Christmas? Are you absolutely losing your mind?"

"Probably," I agree, continuing my walk toward my room. He doesn't stop his pursuit, even as we pass the workshop and several of the staff.

"You can't leave. We need you," he complains, holding the naughty and nice lists with disappointment. Finally stopping, I turn and grip his shoulders.

"I'm going to find my Christmas spirit," I announce, actually believing it's a possibility. Sure, it's a long shot. Something's got to give, though. Living like this forever isn't acceptable. If she can give me what I'm missing, maybe I can grant her a simple wish.

"How do you possibly believe that's doable?"

For the first time in a while, I smile. "I've got this feeling."

"A feeling?" he says with exasperation. "You hate Christmas, Arson. What does this town offer that the North Pole doesn't?"

"Hope," I conclude, and shuffle past him without turning around.

*Dear Mr. Doesn't Respond To My Letters,*

It's day eighteen. I think I'm in over my head.
The idea of love has always been such a dream of mine.
As time goes on, not only with zero response—though
I'm sure you're a busy person—I feel absolutely hopeless.
Maybe love was too far of a reach.
Guess I'll be a little more descriptive.
It'll probably make you run for the hills.
I've never experienced sex. No one has ever touched or kissed me,
Santa. Romance isn't a term in my vocabulary,
but I want to change that.
I want you to help me change that.
I might just need to find peace within the Christmas love I've always
had. Either way, I wish I could know if you are real.
Knowing that could ease the sadness creeping in.
Love sounds so beautiful. Someone to adore you, treasure you, and want
every part of you. Flaws and all, they'd want you.
I'm starting to sound like a broken record. I'll probably not even send
this one. It's a little too sad. Hope this winter is warm and
comforting, Santa. You deserve that.

*My last letter,*
*Sad Unjolly Panda*

# CHAPTER 5

## WHAT CHRISTMAS MEANS TO ME – STEVIE WONDER

## XO

I set down the pen, sealing the letter inside the envelope. Placing it on my nightstand next to my bed, I let go. My heart aches in such a strange way. Is this what true heartbreak feels like? Can someone feel it without ever first experiencing love for themselves?

Picking it back up, I contemplate my choice. Not writing the same address I've done for weeks, I set it down once more. Maybe this one should stay here. Not meet Santa. He might think I'm crazy.

Hell, he probably already does.

I blink the exhaustion from my eyes, heaviness weighing on them as a sleepy promise. The air is warm, soothing, so welcoming to me when the outside is blistering cold.

Snow finally falls, the little flakes gliding down to the ground, decorating the entire town in white. I was hoping to have at least one flurry before Christmas came, and at least Mother Nature has granted my hope. *If she's even real.*

It's the week before Christmas, and I've been a good girl. So good, in fact, that I hope my wishes come true. It's kind of ridiculous to believe in it. Even so, I wrote to Santa to let him know. Over and over. Not that he's responded to a single letter.

I sit on the old couch, green plaid with red and yellow accents. It's hideous, but somehow welcoming. Broken in, sure, but only in the way that tells you many have loved it. And unfortunately, it's the only comfort I've been able to find.

"Santa, I've been so good," I lowly whine aloud, tucking my feet beneath me. My fingers tap the mug of hot chocolate I made while my head rests back against the couch.

The chocolate aroma mixed with peppermint flavoring soothes the disappointment a bit. Sometimes, existing within our means is all we can do. Especially when the sweets taste like I'm melting in a pool of bliss. I'm not necessarily in need of food. Fortunately, human food still tastes delicious.

Turning on the TV, I click to the channel that hosts all the Christmas specials every year and snuggle closer underneath the blanket.

Will Santa bring me a love for Christmas, or ignore my pleas?

I just want someone who will love, cherish, and pleasure me until I can't see straight... is that too much to ask for?

The channel airs *How the Grinch Stole Christmas*, the one with Jim Carrey. While I'm the Cindy Lou of this story, I'm definitely willing to get a Grinch and change his mind.

Anything will do. I'm fairly certain my wishes for happiness are a lost cause.

At some point, I must fall asleep, because I wake to a loud noise outside.

"Santa?"

Generally, loud clangs outside don't exactly mean *friendly*. Yet, I've watched all the human movies, and Santa being noisy is the sign of it. I always wondered if he was real, if the old man with a big heart full of kindness was historical or just a fantasy story people told their kids to get them to behave during the year. Guess I'll find out.

But he never responded to my letters. What if it's a burglar?

Of course, I'd be the first to die in a horror movie. Throwing caution to the wind, I stand and decide to give it to the Fates.

Rushing to the coat closet, I grab my furry coat. Heading toward the door, I stuff my feet into my winter boots and lace them up nicely. It will be bitter with this nightie on and definitely impractical, but it doesn't stop my journey.

Bitter frost meets me as I head out. My teeth chatter as the cold digs into my skin. There's at least six inches of snow, and as soon as I step onto the porch, the crunch brings me such satisfaction. It's a white wonderland. The lights I put outside are glowing beautifully, so vibrant and arresting.

"Santa!" I call out, wondering if he'll respond or if this is a big mistake. There's a rustling of noise and a grunt, but I don't see anyone.

I rush to my garage, my feet crunching the powder beneath me. While the garage door opens, anticipation keeps me warm. My body heats as I do a side-by-side hop dance, excitement being my only mode right now.

Once it's up, I rush inside and grab the ladder. There's only one part of my house that has a safe and flat area. It must be where he went. That or he can magically not fall from sloped roofs.

Practically running, I go to the east side of my house and press the ladder atop it. "Santa, is that you?" I ask again, hoping it's secure enough to the ledge.

No response has concern filling me. Is he hurt? Is the lack of a flat roof giving him problems?

I take the steps too quickly, and before I know it, my feet slip from the wetness. Not only that, but the ladder slides from my roof too, coming toward me as we both fall.

It's as if time slows, my chest rapidly beats, but I'm not falling. How am I still falling?

Looking around me, I try to find the ground and the ladder, and somehow, we're stuck in a frozen state of time. What the hell?

"Xóchitl, why must you be so impatient?" a deep voice booms. The sound sends chills up my spine and I swear my skin tingles. Maybe it's the cold, the bitterness of winter, mixing with the man somewhere behind me.

"I just wanted to see Santa," I respond with a pout. I'm set on my feet, yet despite that, I don't see anyone. Scanning the darkness, all that meets me is Christmas lights and white flurries cascading down in an erratic pattern.

MAEVE BLACK

# CHAPTER 6

## WHAT CHRISTMAS MEANS TO ME – STEVIE WONDER

## ARSON

She's breathtaking.
    Achingly beautiful.
    I didn't expect that. For her to not only steal my thoughts but also for her to not be human. My little Joyful is pink.
Like her letters.

My fingers itch to reach out and touch her, see if she's tangible and not just a figment of my imagination. And, to give in to what I've been wanting to do for days. Sure, that's not what I'm here for. But shit, she's good enough to devour. Maybe she'll taste like candy canes too.

Joyful places her hands on her hips, her mouth a little red from the blistering cold. It's adorable how crimson her nose and cheeks are as a result.

She may not be human, but she's not at all accustomed to this weather, either.

"Are you going to hide forever, Santa?" Her voice is full of sass and desperation, and I've spent every minute since I read the letters, waiting to see if I could meet her and find my spirit again.

I'm above and behind her. Flying. It's nice to allow my wings to stay out and not fear the consequences. I'm not what she sought, not exactly. But the legends of Santa Claus are absolutely not true to me either. Not to any man in my family, matter of fact.

Sure, I give gifts, make toys, and have a factory larger than humanity could understand. But, I'm also *not* human.

I'm something much more...

"I can't believe you stopped time so I wouldn't fall but won't even greet me," she huffs, stomping her little boot atop the ice. She's pouting with her pink little lip sticking out. She looks like a man's wet dream, and I shouldn't be watching her this way.

Her legs are bare, her ass would've been, too, if I hadn't stopped her fall. She's shivering now, and while I want to watch from afar for much longer, to enjoy and pause time to drink her in, I won't let her suffer because of my desires. I'm not that kind of monster.

Finally landing, I stand near her. That doesn't stop her screech and near fall after jumping so high. I chuckle at the way she grips her chest, her little puffs of air sporadic and quick.

"Xó," I rasp, not knowing why my voice dropped so low. Sure, I'm attracted to her. Any being who says otherwise would be a bold-faced liar.

She's literally a cherub, ready for the plucking.

"Santa?" she questions once more, her little dark pink eyebrow rising with questions. I guess that's what they call me, but shit, imagine if she called me by my name?

Specifically, while I took her between her thighs and made her beg... would she like that?

"It's Arson," I correct. Santa is some religious spectacle. Even if it is a shortened version of our last name, Santana. It's not *my* name. Her eyes widen, uncertain and laden with confusion. Her eyes are the pinkest shade, and I wonder if every part of her is pink too.

"No ho, ho, ho? What kind of Santa are you?"

"The only kind you've got," I grumble, wondering if this was truly my best bet. Finding a random person who wants a wish and hoping she'll return the favor.

"You don't look human." It's not a question, simply a statement. She reaches out, her little pink hands with candy cane striped nails are so pleasant and pretty, outstretched for me. I stop her right before we make contact by stepping backward. She's wearing a striped negligée, matching her nails—that would also match my cock—and I'm a fucking mess already.

This is not good.

"I'm not, but no one who has lasted through all the ages could be human, no?" I deflect, needing a *dick*straction.

She nods then shakes her head, closing her eyes. "I just wanted to meet Santa and beg him to give me what I wished for. I wasn't selfish—" she starts then stops, pacing while squeezing her eyes shut. She locks her arms straight and her hands are fisted as if patience evades her. "I just want love."

I nod, thinking of her letters. Yes, it was so specific. A certain love. One I could teach her to find. It's easy to be attractive. She's got those big eyes and a cute pouty face. But a person who would kill for her and would never betray her will be a harder find.

"We should get you inside," I murmur, wanting to push a loose curl behind her ear. I want to touch her, memorize her body, and devour her too. "It's freezing and you shouldn't be shivering like this."

These are thoughts I eradicate immediately. Fuck. I shouldn't be caring for her already. That's not why I'm here. We both have jobs to do.

She glares at me, her eyes narrowing into slits. "You haven't answered my question, are you Santa?"

"Santa is what they call me," I disappointedly grunt, adding an eye roll for emphasis. The untampered part of me wants to tuck her into me and warm her up. Her body shakes but the stubbornness doesn't disappear, if anything the wrinkles in her forehead deepen.

"So, you got my letters?" she questions, her eyes roaming my form. It's not in a sexual way, but almost like she doesn't believe me.

When I nod, she gnaws on her lip. The nervousness she's feeling is visual. She moves from one foot to the other and then continues biting her lip.

"So..." She drags the word out, not looking at me.

I want to smile, laugh, and maybe tilt her chin toward me, but something tells me when I touch her, I'll never want to stop, and neither of us are ready for that.

"Do you always start your sentences with that word?" Her eyes roll so hard and quick that I could easily believe I didn't see it. "Humans must be rubbing off on you."

The way it sounded dirty by my tone of voice and how her cheeks darken lets me know it came out just as sultry as it felt.

Running a hand through my hair, avoiding my horns, I try chuckling away the awkwardness. I didn't mean to but the way her dimples poke through as she laughs at my expense is worth it.

"I'm not a fan of humans, so no," she teases. "And I definitely don't have them *rubbing* off on me." Her eyebrow raises again as if she's silently asking me if I understand.

"They don't seem to like to listen either, though," I challenge, waving to her open door. "They are stubborn and would freeze. And you seem to not like listening too."

She bites her bottom lip and then smirks at me. "I listen," she taunts. "For the right person and for the *right* reasons."

Her innuendo is clear and I feel the collar of my shirt warming with an intense heat. Shit, I've never felt this way before. Whether that's a result of how I low-key stalked her for the last day or she's just *that* charming, I'm losing a battle of wills to be a good guy—and we've only just met.

MAEVE BLACK

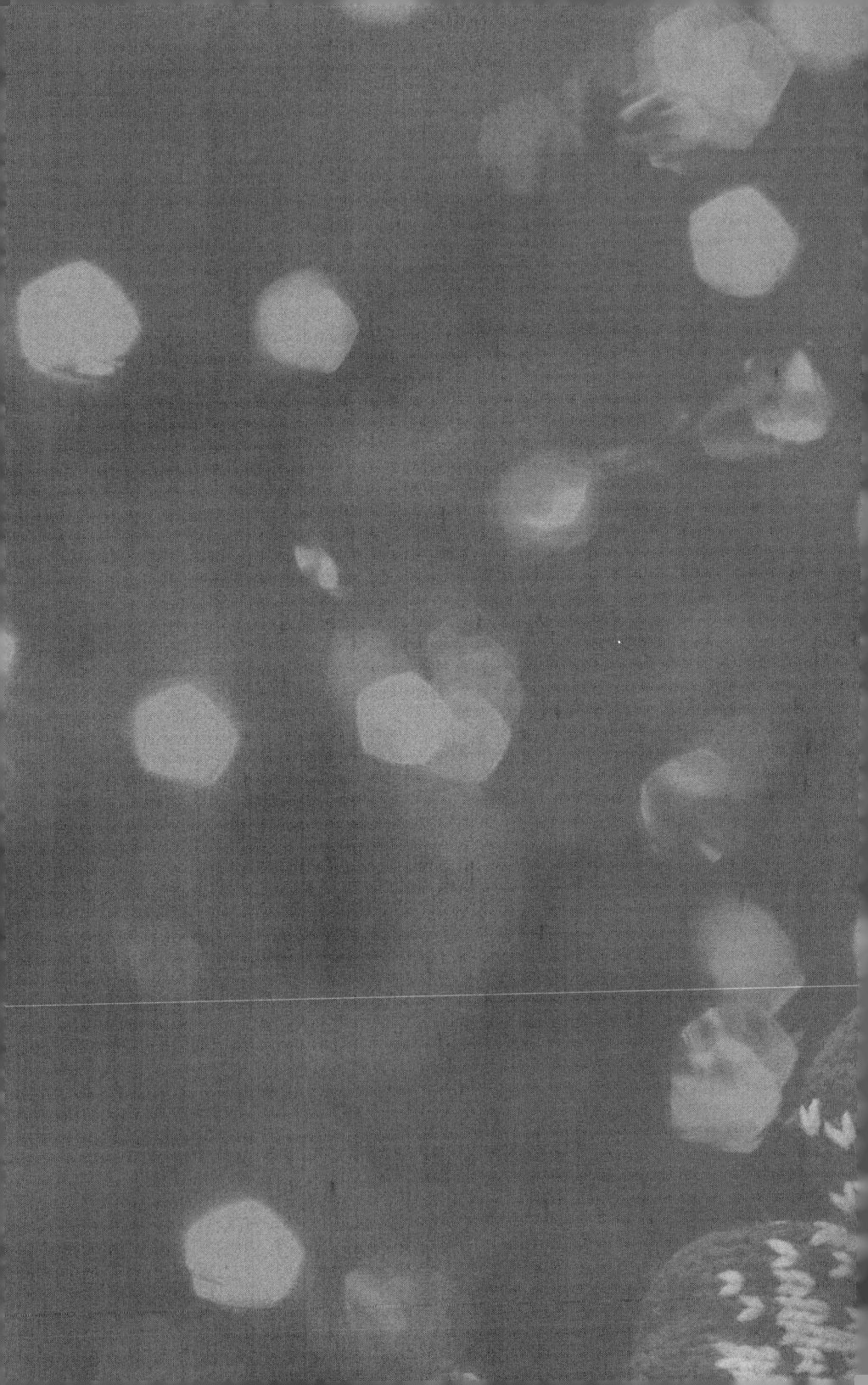

# CHAPTER 7

SNOWMAN — SIA

XO

He's hot as Hades.

My heart hasn't stopped hammering since he hopped out of thin air. While he probably thinks I'm shivering from the cold, I'm not. My skin is melting. It's sweltering with him huddled near me. Plus, I'm shaking because I'm beyond help.

What gets me most is the way he's the reddest kind of red there is. He's got piercings in his bottom lip, and his sharp teeth peek out when he lightly smiles. He's Santa. No wonder they wrote that song, "Santa Baby."

"Inside, right," I finally reply, my throat feeling parched.

His hair is buzzed on the sides, messy on top, and in disarray. Part of me finds it sad that he isn't wearing a Santa costume, but he does don that red hat with white filigree, though. And that's hot as Hades too.

*I think I have the hots for Santa Claus.*

He's decked out in black. *Leather*. Black freaking leather. Ripped jeans, a black tee, and that jacket of leather. He's like a freaking present. No one mentioned Santa being an Adonis. He's so tall and hulking, and I'm basically a mouse next to him.

Sure, I'm taller than average. Five-foot-seven, but he's got to be at least six and a half feet tall, if not taller. He's muscular and charming and I haven't stopped looking at him for long enough to catch my breath.

I'm breathing heavily, I think. Or erratically. I can't really differentiate between the two, but my chest tightens and blackness spots my vision.

Is this what girls feel like when they meet their idols? Because I feel like I'm about to pass out and if this stranger sees me embarrass myself like that, I might not survive it.

"You okay?"

His little smirk reappears and my gaze falls to the piercings again. What else is pierced? *Stop thinking like that, you hussy.*

I can't seem to respond, I'm gasping, I'm... *I'm falling.*

"*Xó?*" His strained voice sooths my anxiety. He sounds like warm peppermint hot chocolate and s'mores by the fire. He's so woodsy and masculine. My body hums as he shakes me. No, don't wake me. *This is the best dream.*

"Hey, please tell me you're okay," he rasps, and his voice sounds distant, concerned. Don't stress, Santa. I've been good, and I'm getting my reward.

He reaches for my hair, then stops before touching it, resting his finger on my jaw. Our skin connects and while I'm not fully cognizant, I am very much aware of the zap. My skin burns, sizzling like it's on fire, and my chest beats so rapidly, I worry I'm dying.

I let out a little whimper when his hand moves away from me.

"Don't go," I whimper. "Please don't go."

"Wouldn't dream of it," he responds, and goddess, I love the sound of his concerned voice. It's so warm and homely. Everything I asked Santa for and didn't even realize.

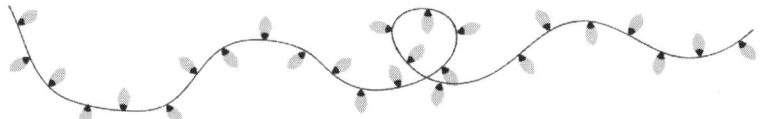

When I wake up, I'm snuggled under my ugly sweater blanket. I'm not on the couch like before. Wait, did I have a spectacular dream?

Sitting up in my bed, my eyes connect with the dark room. Light barely bleeds through my cracked blinds, but it's not sunrise quite yet.

Still in my nightie, I put on my slippers and head toward the kitchen. Nothing a warm cup of coffee won't fix.

"Oh, good. You're awake."

I scream bloody murder at the deep voice coming from the living room. He rounds the doorway and that smirk from my dreams exists in reality now.

"You're real?" The question must catch him off guard because he chuckles, throwing his head back at my expense. The expanse of his throat is so appealing. There's a deep urge to sidle up to him and inhale his spicy aroma.

"Wow. I didn't even let you hit your head as you fell." It's a teasing response, but I want to slap the humor from his handsome face.

Now that I'm not fainting from shock, I take him in. He's really tall, *very* attractive, and has big wings. Holy crap.

"Are you a draegyn?" The words tumble from me and maybe it's rude to ask, especially with their species being gone for centuries in my realm.

He narrows his gaze, his olive-green eyes somehow darker with moodiness. Yeah, I remember that from last night too. The way he holds a kind of world-weary exterior, even while amused with me.

"If I tell you, you've got to tell me what you are," he barters, roaming my body from head to toe.

I point at my own chest. "Is it not obvious?" I laugh, the words leaving me almost sardonically. All Cupids look the same. We're basically all soft features with pastel coloring.

He shakes his head immediately, folding his arms across his wide chest.

He's so muscular and striking, and I can't seem to get over it. *I must shake it off.*

"I'm Cupid. Well, one of them."

His features soften and his eyes widen, too. "Cupid? You are real?"

Now, it's time for me to laugh. "Of course we're real." I roll my eyes at his shock. He's freaking Santa Claus. I guess it's more like Monster Claus at this point, but regardless, if he's real, why is it unfathomable for me to be too?

"Then why can't you find love yourself?" he shoots. It's a direct hit, hurting me where it's most tender. Did he not read my letters? It's not in the cards for me.

My face falls as sadness overwhelms all my senses. He comes closer, reaching for me, but drops his hands before hitting his mark.

"I'm sorry—" he starts, and I cut him off.

"It's okay. It's why I was hoping Santa was real. Cupids don't love. It's not written by the Fates that way." It's such a simple explanation but there's no way to say it differently.

He nods once and then folds his arms once more. "We'll make a deal."

"A deal?" I protest, lightly stomping my foot. "Santa gives without payment, no? Why does it have to be a transaction?"

His signature lip tilt comes and once again brings my eyes to the metal double-looped in his lip.

"I give *children* their wishes for free, Joyful. You're the furthest thing from a child," he emphasizes, gazing at my body. He points behind him toward my couch to follow him, and we both sit, facing each other.

"Okay, get it over with," I grumble. "Tell me the price."

"In exchange of finding you love, you'll help me get my Christmas spirit back."

My face must show my confusion because he closes his eyes with irritation. It's then I notice his eyebrow is also pierced and I hate that I've tucked that info into my pocket for later.

"Christmas spirit? Done."

As if he was expecting an argument, he opens one eye and raises a brow.

"Wait, really?"

"Yeah," I agree, thinking of how much fun it is to enjoy this time of year, especially now. Heck, tonight is the tree lighting ceremony in the center of town. "Christmas is my jam."

"How? You're basically the giver of love and happiness. Christmas is so greedy and full of entitled people."

Now, it's time for my jaw to drop as shock fills me. How can he say that? It's so festive, where kindness comes and is shared everywhere. It's so peaceful and sweet.

"I'm confused," I finally say, closing my mouth. "You're Santa."

He shakes his head with a whispered grievance. "Yeah, and I never asked to be. I'm not even sure why I came. Other than my brother is pretty angry with me, and I've got to get my groove back before the night of Christmas Eve."

"Then let's stop playing around, Monster Claus. Let's find that holiday cheer."

He scrunches his face in disgust and I'm suddenly aware at how anti-Christmas he is like Val. Of course when I agree to fix someone in a genuinely good way, they have to be difficult.

"Okay, then we'll find you love," he resigns himself to it. A flicker of tension fills his shoulders, stiffening them as he stands.

"Wait, but I don't know how to find it."

## CHAPTER 8

### SANTA TELL ME – ARIANA GRANDE

## ARSON

"**W**ait, but I don't know how to find it."

Her words play on repeat for the next two minutes as I blankly stare at her empty living room. For someone who loves Christmas, she's lacking her own cheer.

Back to the topic at hand, I turn to her crestfallen face and decide I'll ask the hard questions first.

"Have you ever fucked someone?" I lay it out there. Sure, sex isn't exactly love. It can come with it, though. For me, it's a way to truly know someone. Knowing people intimately, learning their likes, how they want to be touched, and how they love being fucked… it's phenomenal.

Her cheeks darken, spreading down to her throat, and I can't help but notice the way her chest also flushes.

"I'm taking your embarrassment as an admission that you're a virgin."

Her eyes become wide as saucers and my dick does a little twitch. *I'll teach her, boss.* The stupid traitor. This is not the plan at all.

"This is not what I expected," she squeaks out as she grips her throat in comfort. She's tapping her leg while I stand above her, wondering how experienced she is.

That's not a place my mind should ever wander to, but the thought of her being as innocent as she acts is not something I can pretend to ignore.

"Have you orgasmed?"

"Okay, this is too much." She barely breathes out the words as her hands go from her neck to her chest as if her heart is racing.

I know my heart rate gradually increases as she goes through the motions, but it's definitely the one below the belt.

"I'll take that as a no," I continue, hoping my cock gets the memo. She's off-limits. This is about getting the holiday spirit back not dipping my candy cane.

Even if that sounds so fucking sweet, and she'd probably love the taste too.

"I-I'm—" she stutters, and I want to grip her face, peer into her eyes, and ask her how she wants to get off. Does she like her pussy eaten? Maybe she likes the slow circles and soft clit sucks while my fingers reach for her g-spot.

"Have you ever—"

"Stop!" she hisses, placing her fingers over my lips, pinching them when I attempt to speak. "I've never had sex, no orgasms—not even by my hand—and I've not kissed anyone either." The words tumble out, her innocent little secrets bleeding from her.

When I don't move my lips, she lets them go, and I kind of like them there. Distracted by her sweet scent, the softness of her skin... *Stop.*

"Then we'll start easy," I offer, placing my hands at her hips. The satin material of her baby doll creases beneath my touch, and my claws lengthen. Sucking in a breath, I calm the irrational part of me that wants to be her instructor far too much. But if it's lessons she wants, I'll be an excellent fucking teacher.

"W-what are you doing?" she breathlessly asks. Our faces are far too close, too tempting. She's not wearing that lipstick she always painted her letters with and I really love the shade. It would go lovely with my red and white striped cock.

Closing my eyes, I force myself to focus on anything but the sexual desire I'm feeling. It makes no sense. I've been willingly celibate for ages. No one has even slightly entertained a thought in my mind. Yet this woman I've only just met has me wrapped around her candy cane colored fingers.

"I'm showing you what it feels like to be held," I rasp, hearing my own unsteady emotions. She's drawing me in without trying and I almost wonder if that's what it is to be a Cupid. Maybe they release pheromones. That must be it.

I internally think of the logistics of body chemistry and how Cupids can make random strangers fall in love. That must be the answer. She must be perfuming the air with sex hormones.

"I like it, I think," she whispers, her eyes stuck on my lips. And fuck, I'd kiss her right quick, take her mouth and breathe in her moans.

Dropping my hands as if they're iced over, I step back. "See. Lesson one is done."

She lets out a heavy breath and nods, a small smile peeking from the corner of her lips. "This is going to be great! Let's start your journey?"

I nod, needing my heart and dick to calm the fuck down. She's just a Cupid, a pretty fucking pink love machine.

"Where to?" I ask, knowing that once we leave this place, I'll have to look like an average human. Hiding my wings and skin is the equivalent to going outside naked. The absolute worst unless it's for fucking.

"I think I need a Christmas tree and tonight is the lighting ceremony in the town square!" Her joy has me a tiny bit convinced, but my first reaction is to grumble at it.

"Do we have to?"

She enthusiastically nods. "Oh, absolutely. We're going to make you a jolly man."

"I'd be jollier if I didn't have to hide," I complain, wiggling my wings. Her eyes immediately fall to them. Once her fingers stretch toward me, I put them away quicker than ever before. No. She can't touch them.

That's far too intimate. No partner in the past has touched them, and I won't let some stranger do it right off the bat, either.

"Sorry," she apologizes, pulling her fingers back and hovering them over her mouth. "I shouldn't just touch. I hate when people do that to my hair."

It's so curly, her hair. Rivulets and bouncy curls. They're beautiful and I'd punch any person who dared touch them without her permission.

"It's okay, they're unique."

She nods her head. "You never answered me earlier," she segues into the initial question that brought me to her reality.

"I'm a draegyn."

"I knew it!" she squeals and jumps with excitement. The ones who survived the war of kings abandoned the realm once their numbers dwindled. My father and all his siblings being a part of that.

They came here, and thus Christmas and Santa were born.

"You're so beautiful," she adds when I stay silent. Her eyes seem to glow when she admires me and I'm not sure why the heat overwhelms my system, but I refuse to acknowledge it, regardless.

"Thank you." I run a hand through my hair, trying to avoid eye contact with her.

"Let's head to Pine Hall."

I'm not even going to ask her what that is, but I'm sure it's a fancy name for the forest. Either way, I'm just following her lead.

She stands and heads toward her room. "Just got to change really quick," she embarrassingly squeaks out before closing the door.

I've never wanted Superman's X-ray vision more than I do at this very moment.

MAEVE BLACK

## CHAPTER 9

### LIKE IT'S CHRISTMAS — JONAS BROTHERS

### XO

"Before you hid away your wings, I was going to let you know these people accept the excuse of cosplaying," I explain, holding my peppermint coffee. It smells divine, and I even made Arson a mug of his own.

He hasn't tried it, but I know when he does, his ice-covered little anti-holiday heart will defrost.

Arson's gaze lands on mine as we head to the tree lot. He's currently in a human-like flesh and it's odd to witness. His natural state is much better. He's a deep red, with darker red scales across his cheekbones, arms, and I'm sure other places.

"Really?"

I quickly nod, taking a sip and moaning my happiness. "Yes, that's what I tell them."

His eyes widen and before my eyes, he's shifting into his normal skin, minus the horns and wings. He looks so attractive, and I bite my lip to avoid telling him how good he looks.

"I'm surprised they believe you," he says as we walk down Memory Lane. It's so beautiful now, covered in snow.

"Why? Other than being pink, I'm just a normal not-human."

He lets out a little laugh, shaking his head. "Regardless, we're in a small town."

"But we're near the holidays. There are conventions and events where people dress differently," I argue, shivering a little as we keep walking.

I wore my fleece leggings beneath my Christmas dress, tall boots with ankle warmers, and a puffy jacket. Yet I still have tingles and little chills everywhere. Something tells me it's Arson's doing. My body reacts to him as if I've licked a battery.

I'm going to pretend it's from the peppermint and not being in close proximity to the most handsome creature I've ever met.

"Why aren't you wearing a jacket?" I immediately ask him as I go over my attire. I'm dressed for winter and he's dressed like he's about to jump into a pool. Except, he wears a shirt.

"I'm a draegyn, Joyful. Hot as hell." *Hot as hell is right.*

"Did you just call me Joyful?" I wonder aloud, thinking of the name.

"Yeah, you didn't seem to care last night."

I swallow the dryness in my mouth. He said *last night* like we slept together and not like we've just met.

"We're almost there," I say instead, changing the conversation immediately. His lips tilt and I want to bite them. Eradicating the thought immediately, I quicken my pace.

It's not a long walk. This entire town is only about five miles in circumference, I'm sure. Once the lit-up sign greets us, I'm nearly jumping in joy.

Something about the crisp winter air and the smell of pine wafting in the wind tickles my fancy far too much.

"Howdy!" a man hollers at us and I instantly wave back.

"Looking for a big and fluffy tree!" My excitement warms me from the inside out, and his reciprocated happiness as he guides us through the lot is welcome.

He goes through all the trees, and most are too small. When he notices my slight disappointment, he peers at Arson.

"You look like a sturdy fellow. Maybe you can carry it for the lady?"

"Absolutely not," he responds, and I literally balk, my mouth dropping open.

"Okay, Mr. Grinch. Let's not be rude. I can call a cab."

"To fit one of those?" the man asks, his eyes nearly bulging from his head. The one my sights are on is taller than Arson, wide, and full of pine needles. It's perfect, fragrant, and after we decorate it, it'll be stunning.

"Yes, it'll fit on the roof?" I question aloud, trying to imagine it. Most cabs are cars, especially in a town so small.

"I don't think anyone will have a truck for this," the salesman tries to inform me. He may not know me, but once I put my mind to something, I'll do my best to make the outcome work out in my favor. Especially for the perfect Christmas tree.

"This is the one. I need this one." My voice sounds so small, almost like a beg, and Arson isn't having it. He rolls his eyes and grouses under his breath.

But this is the whole point of finding his Christmas spirit, forcing him to witness it, even if it's only through my own eyes.

"You are carrying this tree back to the house," I demand, pointing at him while putting my booted foot down. Arson turns to me with two raised eyebrows and folded arms. "We have a deal." I tack it on for good measure, but it's true.

He lets his head fall backward as he expresses the loudest sigh known to monsters. "Fine. We'll take it."

The older man appears to be both shocked and concerned. "You've made your wife very—"

"Whoa, whoa. Just colleagues," I correct. Arson smirks, and part of me thinks he's planning to do something mischievous.

"She's just a little shy. Aren't you, Joyful?" Arson taps my chin with one finger and I swear to the goddess as our eyes connect and his finger lingers, I melt. "We'll get the tree," he says, and his voice sends all the tingles across my body.

I'm not sure what they mean, but I like them. A lot.

MAEVE BLACK

# CHAPTER 10

## WONDERFUL CHRISTMASTIME – PAUL MCCARTNEY

# ARSON

**W**hy did I agree to this torture?

My legs work as I cart this huge-ass tree on my back. If we were more hidden, I would've flown with it, but as it is, it's prickly as hell and I'm stuck overexaggerating the weight to appease the old man.

I look ridiculous, I'm sure. Hunched over, carrying a massive tree, with a little giggling woman next to me, so happy I'm unsure how she could ever frown.

"I thought draegyns were strong," she teases, and I grunt my disapproval of her heckling. Sure, make fun of the monster carrying your beloved tree…

"You know, I can literally breathe fire, Joyful. Might want to be sweeter," I taunt right back, and her face falters a little.

"You wouldn't."

"I would," I grump, blowing out a little puff of smoke. Her eyes widen and she gnaws on her pretty pink lip.

"Where's the Christmas spirit in that?"

Her gaze narrows, calling me out on my saltiness. She's not wrong, but I like to see the combative side of her. Maybe there's more than simple innocence behind her doe eyes.

Once we round the first corner, away from lurking humans, I stand taller. Damn, this makes such a difference to my posture. She smiles and from the corner of my eye, I swear I can see her do a little skip.

I think part of her fun is torturing me. She just doesn't realize that I'm more than willing to give it back, tenfold.

By the time we're back, my plan is in motion. It's burning inside me like the flames barely kept beneath the surface. It's thriving there, a festering ache, and while half of it is for my amusement, seeing her fall apart beneath me sounds too enticing to ignore.

Setting down the tree, I wait for her to grab the stand for it. She places it on the ground, putting a pink and silver skirt around it. Lifting and lowering the tree into the hole, I make sure it's steady while she twists the pins.

"Hold it while I drill them deeper," I instruct and shit, the innuendos could write themselves. She does as she's told and I twist the screws until I hear them crack the wood.

Once that's done, it stands tall, nearly touching the chandelier. This room is lofty, probably around ten feet tall, but the chandelier hangs closer to eight feet. The tree is brushing on the higher end over seven. We might not be able to get a star up top.

Reality hits me and I note that it's been years since I've set up a tree. Warmth gathers in my chest and I just know it's a brief flicker of optimism.

"I have all the pink, silver, and gold ornaments!" Joyful practically yells, her happiness not faltering. It's nice seeing her at absolute peace with this tree.

She grabs a tote, and I can't resist looking at her as she bends over. I'm hopeless and perverted, shit.

I mentally reprimand myself before she comes over. Her eyes nearly glow with excitement as she pulls out the most Barbie-looking pink ornaments. They're covered in glitter and little diamonds. It's so fitting for her personality but also adorable because it's what she wanted.

"Do you like them?" Her eyes are half-lidded and almost shy. Like she's worried I'll toss them away.

I rotate one in my hand, peering at the way the glitter sticks to my skin. "Other than the shiny shit that'll never leave any crevice, I think they're cute."

That seems to satisfy her, because she's smiling large enough to bring her cute dimples forward. "Want some more peppermint coffee?" she offers, hopping around like she's already consumed far too much.

"I didn't get the chance to try it," I admit. It's not that I didn't get the chance, it's more that the taste of peppermint sets me off.

When your cock is literally candy cane striped and can curve inside a person, hitting their pleasure spot... peppermint flavors mean something different.

To me, it's a kink. All things candy cane taste like me. That shit turns me on.

"Oh, I'll make you more!" Without waiting for my refusal, she practically dances into the kitchen. As if it couldn't get more festive, she turns on her speaker and Christmas music bleeds out.

"Wonderful Christmastime" by Paul McCartney hits my ears and I smile. It's the type of nostalgia one chases this time of year, and it immediately relaxes my shoulders. Sitting on the couch, I wait for her to come back. Putting up ornaments without her seems completely odd.

And for some reason, I want to experience these moments with her, watching as joy seeps into me from her.

A few minutes later and she's walking in with two mugs. One has a candy cane handle and the other has a tree.

I reach for the tree, not needing my dick to make an appearance during this. I literally met her less than a day ago and I'm already getting far too ahead of myself over what isn't mine to claim.

"Here you are," she offers with the biggest grin. "I made sure to add the peppermint sprinkles. They're delectable."

She seems too fucking proud of herself, and if she only knew what this was doing to me, she'd probably rethink this. Hell, I'm trying to think of ways to not take a sip. No one needs a feral draegyn rutting into them.

It's sick of me to have such an addiction to this flavor. I try to set mine down, but her gaze infiltrates my view.

"Aren't you going to try it?" she prods, taking a drink of her own. She lets out a moan and fuck, I can't do this.

I'm supposed to be a mature adult. Respectful.

Once again, I attempt to set it down and a frown mars her face. "You don't like peppermint, do you?"

Her face falls as she thinks she's done something wrong, so I save face and take a sip. And fuck, it's so good. It's sweet and warm. The coffee is the perfect blend, a little strong but smooth as hell.

"Delicious," I rasp, trying to control the way my cock inflates. Every time I've had peppermint has been in a sexual situation. I'm not sure how to avoid it.

"You like it?" Her face lights up and I swear my balls ache at the way she's as addicted to the flavor as me.

"I do," I confirm, taking another drink. To hell with kinks. I can survive this.

She makes this little happy sound and I'm storing that shit for later. "Peppermint is my favorite," she confirms, licking some foam off the top of her coffee. "I could eat it all the time."

Ah, shit. There goes my fucking control.

"Why's it your favorite?" I ask, only torturing myself further. She takes a drink, a little red sprinkle touching her lip.

"It has always drawn me in. It's why I love all things candy canes." She still hasn't licked the sprinkle from her lip and I can't avoid my craving.

Not anymore.

Not as she stares at her nails, the striped ones.

I reach forward, unable to hold back. With my thumb, I swipe at her lip, and it startles her. She hops and makes a squeak.

"W-what are you doing?"

Much like earlier, she's questioning me with a stutter.

"Scared I'm going to kiss you, Joyful?" I'd love to. I'd love to taste the peppermint on her tongue and find out if she tastes as sweet as her perfume. Maybe she's sweeter, addicting, just like I've been imagining.

She shakes her head, but it's too late. I'm leaning in. "You should be," I rasp, kicking my ass at how addictive she's becoming.

It really hasn't been long.

She presses toward me, closing that distance I've barely been keeping, and I literally growl as the taste of peppermint invades my senses.

She's so succulent and I've got a craving. Tentative presses of my tongue brush against the seam of her mouth and she pushes in closer, allowing me access.

My cock feels like a stiff pole, and I fucking hate that I've already caved. I'm teaching her, though. That's what we agreed on, right?

She whimpers as my tongue teases her with light little strokes. Her body shakes a little and I grip her waist to keep her close. As I'm doing that, she must forget the mug in her hand, because it spills all over me.

It's not hot—not to me, at least—but it startles me enough to pull back. Her kiss-swollen lips look absolutely wrecked, and the blush darkening her skin has me standing up.

I need to walk the fuck away. This isn't the plan.

"Bathroom?" I ask, clearing my throat of all tension. Her eyes fall to my tented jeans, and I don't even cover myself up. Partly because it's more embarrassing to pretend I'm ashamed, and the other is my pride and greed. I want her to see how big it is, and I hope she wants to experience it.

*No, you stupid fuck. No.*

"Down the hall and to the left," she directs, but her eyes haven't left where they were last. I chuckle and that seems to disrupt her awe, but her mouth opens and she hurries to hide it with her cute little hand.

    I've realized a new kink is to be added. A size complex. Because she's tiny and I'm huge, we'd look fucking great together.

MAEVE BLACK

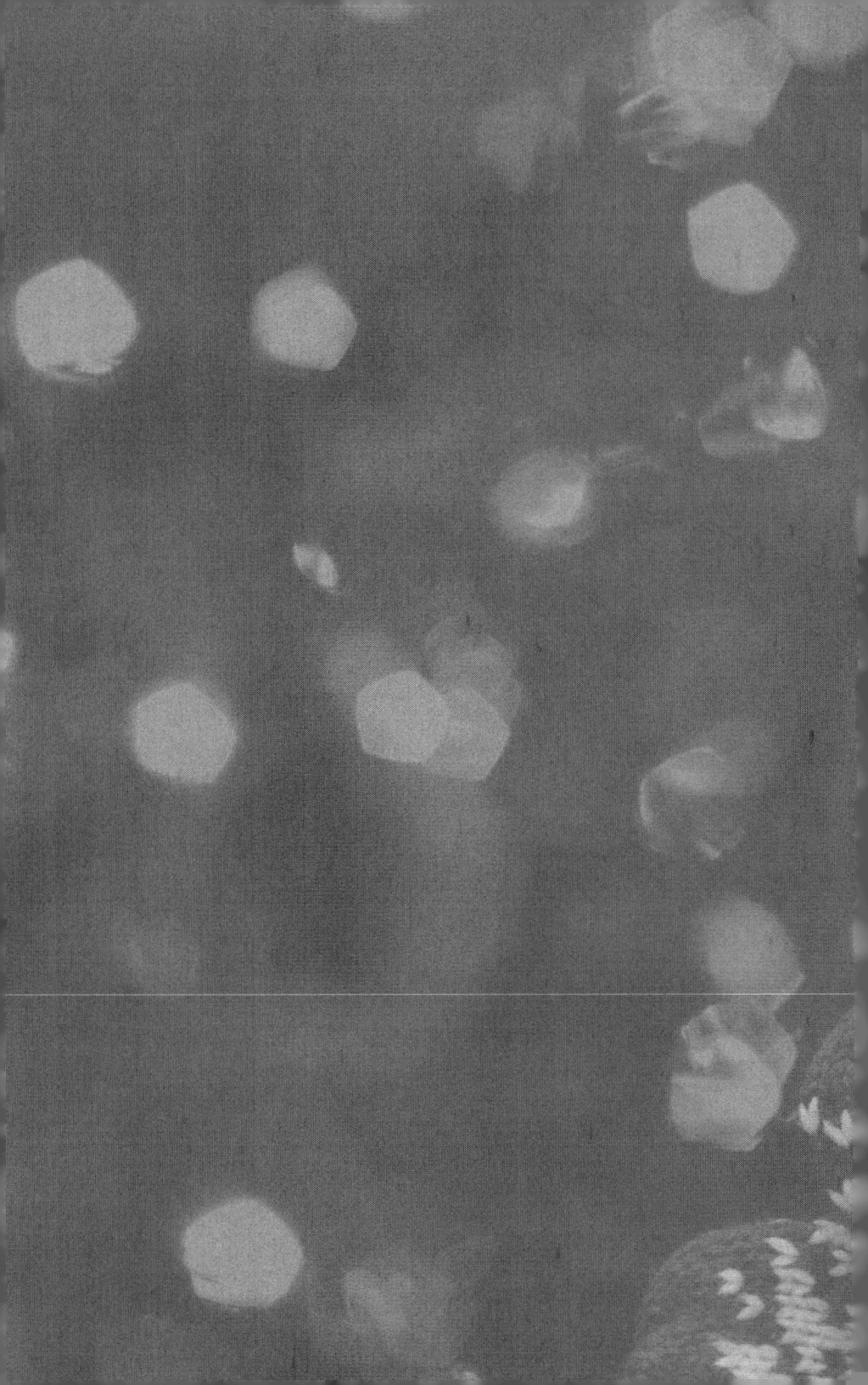

# CHAPTER 11

LAST CHRISTMAS – LOVELESS, DOWNER INC., KELLIN QUINN

## XO

What just happened?

I brush my lips, they tingle against my fingertips. The swollen feeling is abnormal. Are all kisses so fierce and tangible, like they're meant to last forever?

He tasted of peppermint and sweet coffee when our mouths met and I can't think of a better flavor to envelop my taste buds.

Should I ask him to teach me how he did that tongue thing? How I felt like my insides were melting while also being so distracted by the way he stroked me, too?

I didn't realize lessons would be this fun or this beneficial to me. He's an apt teacher, the way he makes sure I'm surprised with his lessons. It's like he wants a raw reaction and not the nervous wreck I'd be if it were planned far ahead.

Standing up, I go into the kitchen and grab a washrag. Most of the coffee spilled on Arson, not my couch. Just in case, though, I'd rather not have stinky milk for later.

Warming the cloth under the running water, I think about what I can have us do until the tree ceremony tonight.

Unfortunately, my mind doesn't go to safe options.

Would he teach me to kiss better? I'm sure he felt my inexperience when our mouths were together, and I was unsure of what to do.

After soaking it, I head back to the living room, cleaning the couch where the littlest of drops hit. It's now wet, but maybe it won't be too noticeable.

"I think my pants are done for," Arson's voice hits my ears. It's so soft. Turning my head in his direction, he has a stoic expression.

"I can wash them," I offer. "Unfortunately, I'm fairly short on men's clothing."

It's not inaccurate. I barely expected to stay here myself. If not for the already stocked dresser in the main bedroom, I'd be screwed.

He unbuttons his pants and I wave a hand in front of my face. "Whoa, there." A chuckle escapes him and shuffling meets my ears as I try to turn away.

"Never seen a naked man before, hmm?"

I shake my head. "You're not exactly a man," I grumble, thinking of how much I'd like to peek through my fingers to see him.

"That, I'm not. Do they not have a porn equivalent of monsters?" His tone is light and full of curiosity, but shame licks my skin.

There is.

There is a monster porn industry. It's not something I've witnessed myself, but my sisters speak about it being hot. I'm sort of jealous. I never got to experience it myself.

While Cupids don't find love, all of my siblings are sexually active. Finding out that tidbit scarred me for life.

How am I the only one unaware of sex and pleasure?

"I'm taking that as a yes." When I don't move back toward him, he touches my shoulder. "I'm dressed. Luckily for you, I have backup trousers."

"I wouldn't call that luck," I mutter under my breath. Instead of calling me out, he offers a playful grin. "I didn't see you carry anything inside?"

"Ah, but you fainted. I brought in my to-go bag."

I finally peek through two fingers and see him standing in a t-shirt and jeans. Much like his last outfit.

"At least one of us preps. I'm not good at that. I'm more of the spontaneous type." He eyes me up and down, and my skin flushes at the way his perusal is far too slow.

"I think chaotic energy fits your personality perfectly," he argues. When I'm staring at him for a second too long, he notices. "Got something on your mind, Joyful?"

"Was I bad?"

He raises an eyebrow, confusion resting between his brows. "What do you mean?"

He's going to make me spell it out for him and I might die of embarrassment at this point. "Kissing. Was I... bad?"

I hide my face behind my hands once more, wanting the ground to split and swallow me whole so I don't have to witness his expression. That's why he left. He was so disgusted that he needed to rethink this alliance.

Like my siblings, he'll probably be annoyed and want to tease me for my inexperience. That's what they do. They laugh that I've never kissed someone.

Of course, I didn't know we could until recently.

It's not my fault that rules are simply suggestions to them. I've always been the good girl. Getting my job done fast and early, making sure there's no misstep or laziness on my part.

But they're the true reckless ones. They do nothing linear and go with what makes them happiest. I'm super jealous of that. That they can just separate their wants and desires from our duties.

Warmth spreads through my body as his hands touch my own. It's sweltering, the way my body reacts to his. Being this close to him has me feeling like a puddle of goo. Is this normal? Have I been missing out on touch this long for no reason? If all touch feels this way, I've held out on myself and that's not fair.

Arson's a new sensation I've only allowed myself to dream of. I know after this, when he finally leaves, I'll definitely be making sure touch is a constant in my future.

He peels my hands from my face, heating my skin in his wake. His eyes are green, so deep and serpent-like, but I find myself enamored and not the least bit scared. Then there's his lips, with those two metal hoops and sharp canines, they have me stunned stupid.

"You were far from bad, Joyful," he confesses, something deeper within his words. Sure, he probably kisses so many people. He wouldn't lie just so I'll continue with this charade, right?

"But that was my first kiss," I whisper conspiratorially. It's hard for me to believe that he's not even the littlest bit glossing over my lack of skills.

"Yeah, and you allowed me to lead. You followed me, listening to the movement and chemistry between us," he explains.

"I don't understand." He shakes his head briefly, his face full of many emotions where I can't pinpoint a single one. "Will you show me how to do it right?"

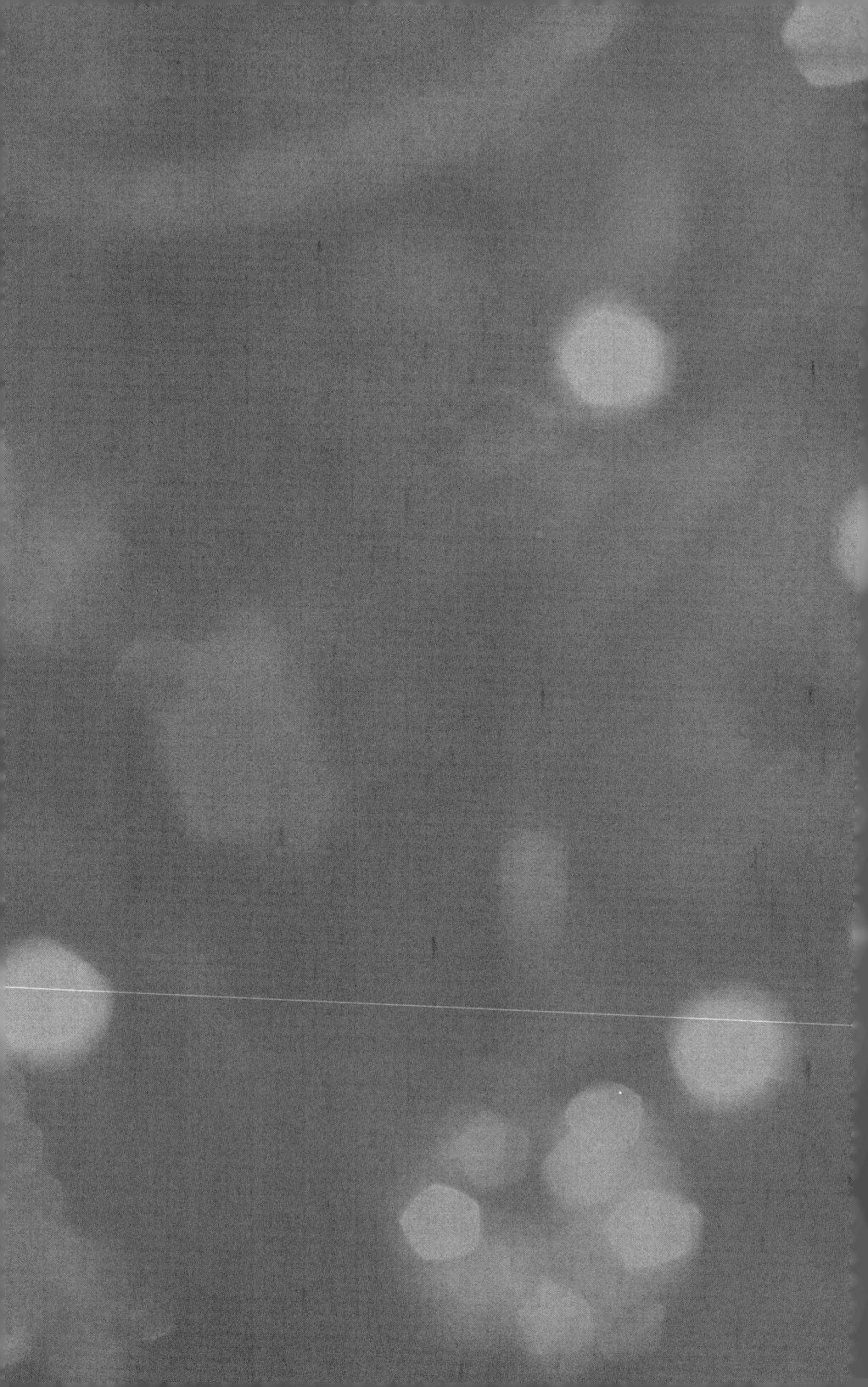

# CHAPTER 12

### UNDERNEATH THE TREE – KELLY CLARKSON

## ARSON

"Will you show me how to do it right?"

Does she not realize what she's doing, and what her words and questions do to me? My mouth dries up at her request. This teaching shit has to end. Already.

It hasn't even been a day and I've already fought an erection and the need to truly illustrate what to do to her. I want to bend her over—demonstrate exactly what her clit is and how good it feels when my tongue flicks it perfectly.

She'd love it, the way she would melt from the constant battle of my mouth between her thighs as I devour what's begging for my lessons.

"Yes," I quickly respond, knowing once we give this up and she finds love, I'm fucked. I was never a strong man, and this only further proves that sentiment. She has me buckling for her easily. Twenty-four hours in, and I'm ready to dive in.

She blinks slowly, and there's no way she knows what that doe in the headlights expression does to me.

My hands slide to her jaw, tenderly cupping her face as our eyes stay locked in a bubble of untapped tension.

Tilting her neck to the side, I lean in, breathing in that delectable scent she left me with in each letter. "You smell like pure sugar." And fuck, she does. Sweet, feminine, and something I want to devour.

She shivers beneath my touch, the heat of my breath no doubt giving a temperature type play.

"Arson," she whispers. A promise or a plea, which one, I'm unsure. Either way, it has me near folding for her. I want to take her throat, suck and leave marks. Bite into her and make her mine.

That's not what I'm here for, so I back up a little to breathe some sanity into my brain.

"When I go for your lips, tease me," I instruct, pressing against her delectable mouth. She whimpers at the contact, her knees buckling. I wound my arm around her waist, pulling her chest against mine.

Tentatively, her tongue traces my bottom lip, stopping at my piercings. My cock throbs as she playfully traces them, tugging with her teeth soon after.

The grunt that leaves me as she bites my lip right after is feral, desperate. I suck in a breath through my nose, only to be greeted by that succulent scent she gives off. Fuck, fuck, fuck. She's a dream. She has to be.

This is unreal.

Her tongue presses against my lips and I allow her entrance. It doesn't take her any time to gain confidence, taking over.

She's so innocent, inexperienced, but in a sweet way. Her exploration is gentle but direct. When her tongue reaches my canines, she licks each one.

I growl deep in my chest, wanting to press them into her and draw blood. Nevertheless, I hold back, breathing out of my nose, pretending I'm not molten lava for this woman.

She dances on my tongue, hitting my ridges before abruptly pulling back.

Her glossy eyes widen, cute and worried. Automatically, my mouth tilts with amusement.

"For pleasure," I rasp, feeling the deepest of my draegyn voice at this moment. I'm seconds away from throwing this stupid teaching thing away and kidnapping her, tying her with ribbon, and fucking her slow.

She bites her bottom lip and whimpers. It's so submissive in the way her eyes reach up, looking through her lashes. I hate how affected I am and how much it has to do with her and not a simple need for sex. She intrigues me in a way that makes little sense.

"Was that... *good*?"

"Does my Joyful need praise?" I tease, leaning in to nip her lip. She makes the cutest sound and a small smile forms on her lips. A simple nod tells me I've got a lot to learn about her. "It was perfect, Joyful. Hot as fuck."

Her face blooms red, and I can't resist the urge to drag my thumb against her cheek. Soon, I'll have her using the words that mortify her now.

She'll be descriptive with what she wants, and I swear I'll kneel at her fucking altar as she pleads for it.

"Aren't we supposed to go to the tree ceremony or whatever it's called?" I ask, praying to break the tension. A little tit for tat. She's supposed to bring me holiday spirit and in return, I'll find her love.

I've got to get on that.

"Oh, yes! We've got a little more time. If you want to..." She pauses, hiding her face. "If you want to give me more lessons?"

It's so hopeful and heated, like she also doesn't understand the burning between us, but can't seem to resist it either.

My balls ache for release, to fill her. I'll definitely have to excuse myself, jerk one or two out, so I'm no longer a liability.

"Sit," I instruct, and I don't have to tell her twice. She sinks to the floor next to her tree. Now decorated, it looks like a perfect depiction of her.

"Good girl," I praise, tilting her chin up at me. She shivers and seems to melt under my touch. I lower to the ground, folding my legs. Her eyes don't leave me, but follow every move.

Tapping my lap, I gesture for her to follow. "Sit on Santa's lap and tell him what you want for Christmas."

Her gaze flashes with heat and she bites the inside of her cheek as she scoots over to me. Once on my lap, she stiffens. Whether from fear or embarrassment, I'm unsure.

I place a hand on her lower back and she nearly jumps from the pressure. "Relax." Her body slouches just the slightest, and she melds into me.

"Such a good listener, aren't you?"

She peers up at me, hopeful, and subtly nods. I press my thumb into her chin, fighting every urge to keep pushing both of our limits here.

Guidance. Practice. Those are the two things she wants. Not me taking advantage of the situation at hand.

Men love when you want them, and whether or not she's aware of how she's showing me she does, it's addictive.

"What do you want for Christmas? Be specific, Joyful."

She wiggles a little on my lap, unknowingly making me harden at the simple movement. Jesus fucking Christ.

"I want love, Santa," she states it like it's a shopping list, and I immediately shake my head in disapproval.

She juts her lip out as if she doesn't understand where she went wrong. I tilt her jaw, exposing that pulsing vein in her throat. Somehow, it steadies me.

"Is that all you want?" I rasp, leaning toward her. "The simple concept of love?"

She shivers and lets out a little sound she pretends didn't escape her lips. I pull back, staring at her nervous lip biting, wanting to distract her.

"There's more," Joyful concedes. She takes no time to cover her face, but I take those hands and hold them above her head. The pout and sass come in full force at that, her eyebrows drawing inward with a mini scowl.

It's adorable.

"If there's more, be specific."

Immediately, she shakes her head, her eyes widening. She knows what I want. What words I'm searching for. Until she gives them to me, we'll stay locked in this sweltering embrace.

Her eyes seem to dilate as she ponders her choices, and I watch her, enjoying the internal battle.

"I want to be loved," she begins, and as I raise an eyebrow to reprimand her, she continues, "but not the easy kind that I offer others. Not one that's immediate. I want something passionate that I feel down to my toes. Where my eyes roll back as he pleasures me and my entire body flames with yearning."

Both my eyebrows rise at her avoidance of explicit words while also telling me exactly what I want to hear. "So Joyful wants soul-shaking orgasms? Check."

"I want him to know every inch of my body, so when I'm needy, he can tell me exactly what I want just by seeing my expressions."

"Mind reader? Check."

She smacks my chest at that, giving the sassiest side-eye. "Think you can find him for me? I know it's only been one day, but I think I'm a quick study."

A jerkiness against my rib cage has red filling my veins. Jealousy. That's what it is. Draegyns claim for life. Even I know this. My draegyn can't claim her, though. She's not ours to have.

"I think the deadline is kind of short for us both, but yeah. We'll find your happily ever after."

As I say the words, I know I won't be able to be here to witness it. I know my magic works well. It's not a science, our family retains gifts and the ability to make things happen without reason. So, I'm sure I'll be able to follow through.

I'm just reluctant to watch it unfold.

Standing, I bring her with me. "You're definitely a talented student, I think it's time for you to teach me. Help me understand why I've lost my way."

Her face lights up with excitement, and I set her down so she can let out that energy. She's so gleeful, jumping up and down. If I could bottle up her feelings and experience them the way she does, there would be no lack of soul inside me.

Maybe she's the key.

Or maybe, just fucking maybe, I'm not meant to be the man in red.

MAEVE BLACK

# CHAPTER 13

## WE THREE KINGS – ANTHEM LIGHTS

## XO

By the time we walk to the town square, I'd have assumed my body would have calmed. It hasn't. If anything, it seems warmer and warmer as time passes. I'm not sure what it's from, but I have an inkling it's to do with the draegyn who knows how to kiss.

Arm in arm, he escorts me to the massive tree. It's so big and burly. They have the entire town help decorate the bottom. Everything else, they pay people to do with huge cranes.

"That thing is inhuman," Arson says, expelling a surprised huff. Him not noticing it when we got my tree is almost humorous.

"It's not humanly, anyway. Trees are woody plants." In Darchon, they have memory and can communicate. A part of me believes the human realm trees do the same.

We walk toward the mayor, where he stands with boxes of ornaments. There are so many and they're all massive. At least twice the size of my biggest ornament.

"Here you are," the mayor offers me one. It's green and disappointment touches me a little by it. I'm not sure why pink is an obsession of mine, but it is.

The next one he hands to Arson is pink, and before I can ask him to trade, he switches them. "Pink is definitely your color, Joyful."

My mind travels back to earlier, when he forced me to sit on his lap and admit my wants. I think he knew mine were going to be the PG-13 ones and not the crass ones he anticipated.

Either way, thinking about how I told him I want someone who reads me comes back to mind. He knows I like pink, yet we've only just met. It gives me hope that when we find my love, he'll know, just like Arson does.

"Everyone, everyone!" the mayor announces, his voice booming over the loudspeaker. Everyone's gathered, their hands together or huddled close. Some peer at each other with that lovey-dovey expression I know so well, and others have pure excitement on their faces, but happiness surrounds the entire area.

"I'm so grateful for the opportunities that happen every year in Mistletoe Grove, but this year especially has been kind. Santa will come to town soon, and I hope you're all on the nice list!"

I twist to stare at Arson and he's already looking at me with humor. I'm sure it's because Santa's already here, but I beam brightly at him.

"Each of you got an ornament, and I'm hoping we can all surround the tree and put it on at once. Then, once we're done, we can sing some carols and drink some cocoa."

Nods and jumps of joy happen and there's something so warm and comforting about this moment. When I glance back at Arson, there's a sparkle in his green eyes that wasn't there last night when we first met.

Already, I can tell he's feeling the vibes here. It's a magical place. Without thinking too hard, I snap my fingers, bringing a sprinkle of snow with us. Once I start the weather process, it doesn't stop. I can only nudge it to come in the way I want.

Hopefully Mother Nature understands this one.

Snow cascades down a few minutes later, the flakes big and crystal-like. People hoot and cheer as they reach their hands up.

"At the count of five, let's hang our ornaments!"

"One, two…" the mayor counts and before he hits one, my hand hovers over the branch. Arson grabs my face and kisses me senseless. There's clapping and yelling but I'm not sure what is causing this, but my entire system has gone into shock.

Heat fuels me, and I take the opportunity to press my tongue against his lips. He nips at me and my eyes fly open.

Drawing back, he's smirking, and my hand still hovers over the branch. I hurry to place my ornament, hoping no one else notices the distraction.

All the people here seem so zoned in on the lights and when I look upward, seeing all the colors and ornaments lit up in the night, emotion clogs my throat.

This never gets old.

Whether I stop by this beautiful town or stay for longer, the tree lighting ceremony is always one of my highlights.

"It's so beautiful," I let out.

"It truly is," Arson agrees before the crowd sings "O Christmas Tree." I hum along with them as Arson holds my hand, leading me around people. The snow falls faster now, still massive flakes that light the sky in white.

My entire body feels like it does after I drink too much of the boozy eggnog, and it's such a welcome feeling.

"Where are you leading me?" He doesn't stop or answer me, just drags me away from the crowd. His eyes fill with something I've been hoping would come out.

It's what he's searching for, even if it's only slight. Maybe he doesn't even know it's there yet, but the Christmas joy he's seeking is in those green eyes of his.

We travel across the bridge toward Candy Cane Lane. Yes, much like the mall one, this is lit up with candy canes. It's where they turn on the entire city's decorations, and somehow Arson must know this.

He slows down when we hit the entrance. Standing off to the side is an older gentleman and a cart that reads *St. Nick's Cocoa.*

"Ho, ho, ho!" the man hollers, his red nose and cheeks visible as he smiles widely. He wears a red Santa hat, a plaid jacket, and rocks a handlebar mustache that reminds me of all those Christmas movie dads.

"Hello," Arson responds at the same time I give a joyous, "Hi!"

"We'd like two of your cocoas," Arson requests, flicking his wrist out of sight and creating money out of thin air.

*That can't be legal.*

He puts a big chocolate-looking ball into paper mugs, handing one to each of us. "They're cocoa bombs," he explains. Before handing us the cups, he adds a stirrer. "Make sure you give them enough time for the peppermint to dissolve and then use the stirring stick. It'll taste like pure joy."

Beaming at him, eagerness fuels me to lead Arson along the path. The first portion has so many lights. All the bushes, trees, and fences from head to toe are decorated. There are blow-up Santas, reindeer, and even some Grinch-themed ones added in.

"I'm more like him than him," Arson comments, pointing at the Grinch and then the average depicted one.

"So, you're saying you *are* Monster Claus. Maybe next year, I'll write 'Dear Monster Claus' instead of writing random messages, not knowing what to call you."

A chuckle greets me, one so boisterous his head falls back. Watching his throat work as he humors me, I find myself wanting to know what the crook of his neck smells like.

He's indescribable. Masculine and warm, and I think there's a hint of cinnamon added to the bunch. There's no way he doesn't smell the best.

"You think you'll be needing me next year?"

"Absolutely," I respond immediately. "It'll be our thing. I'll send a letter and you'll fly down and entertain me." His face falls at the end and I wonder what ruined his happiness. Maybe he doesn't want to see me after this and that thought bothers him.

"I don't think you'll need me after this Christmas, Joyful."

*Joyful.* He's called me that numerous times, but this is the first time it's sounded forlorn, like he's mourning the small friendship we've created.

If that's what we're calling this.

Friends don't kiss, I don't think.

He pauses his pursuit, stirring his drink. Silence being our only companion at the moment, my mind wanders. I want to tell him we'll set some type of tradition for us, that we can make this a seasonal thing. Maybe we can do something for Valentine's Day. It could be us being addicted to the lights and cocoa, and maybe some conversation hearts and cheesy Valentine's Day cards. Realistically, I know it's not possible.

He'll eventually find a person to love and then we'll both be too awkward to have a friendship. My stomach churns at the thought of him finding happiness and not being able to experience it alongside him.

Shaking off the depression promising to drown me, I point at the reindeer lineup. "Are the songs true?" I question, wondering if they truly hated and bullied Rudolph. I would be far too sad if that were the truth.

"Not exactly," he answers with that same sadness from before. "They're not reindeer. Only when we fly over big cities. When we're across the oceans, they're in their normal forms."

"What are their normal forms?"

"Drakes. But not shifters like us. I'm as draegyn as it gets. They're more like the actual dragons from lore. They're mythical beings who choose to help me every year."

"Wow," I mutter in awe, wondering if I'll ever get to meet them.

"They're quite amazing," he comments, and we continue our walk, holding hands and sipping our drinks. Every time we pause at a new light shape, we talk about how it matches his reality and I feel like movies are the worst depiction.

They're the equivalent of fantastical stories you tell children at night to make them go to sleep. Something to pass the time or trick them into a false sense of safety.

# MAEVE BLACK

## CHAPTER 14

### WIT IT THIS CHRISTMAS — ARIANA GRANDE

## ARSON

After the walk in the park, I carried her home. Her exhaustion made her unsteady on her feet. As we journeyed back, she fell asleep in my arms. I tucked her in, wanting to hold her for so many moments longer.

It's the morning after and my mind's already wandering.

When she's near me, I struggle to not want her. It's becoming a problem. But I felt it last night, the tug of hope.

It's small, just a little flicker, but it's enough to keep me going. It's enough to keep me here. Maybe it's just Xó. Her wants and desires rub off on me, bringing me what little Christmas spirit is out there.

"I almost wondered if you'd be here," she says sleepily as she walks to her fridge. Like clockwork, she grabs the heavy whipping cream, caramel, and a little thing of peppermint flavoring over to the coffee maker.

It's already brewing, the sound comforting as we dance around the kitchen, almost practiced. Her messy bedhead and sleepy expression will comfort me for years to come. There's no doubt in my mind that the visual of her in her night shorts and camisole, along with her charming tired eyes, will haunt me in the best way.

"Where would I go, Joyful?"

Her gaze softens, and I want to move her curls from her face so I can see her eyes perfectly. They're so expressive, telling me everything before her lips move.

"Anywhere but here, Monster Claus."

The name is growing on me. I prefer it over Santa for sure.

"What's on today's agenda?" I question, knowing exactly what lesson I'm planning on teaching her.

She's going to have her first orgasm tonight and witnessing it myself will easily be the best night of my life.

Blinking slowly, she doesn't respond. However, she rubs her eyes before giving me her full attention.

"I think we should build a snowman," she suggests. It's such a childlike experience, but I don't feel the immediate refusal spilling from my lips.

Guess that's changing.

"Sounds frosty," I rebut, but don't deny it. She notices and a small smirk appears on her face.

"You didn't grumble, grumpy. Losing that edge?"

I grip her waist, noticing how easy it is for me to do, it's comfortable, like I'm meant to be doing it.

"I think we both need some coffee, or we'll both be grumpy."

She giggles lightly, moving toward the carafe. Lifting it, she pours the liquid into two mugs. One that says, *Ho, Ho, Ho!* The other says, *This isn't the only white stuff I make.* People could take that in one of two ways. That they're discussing cum or with the snowflakes they're discussing coke. I'll go with the former because it's comical.

She uses a candy cane as a stirrer instead of a spoon, pouring all the ingredients before topping it with whipped cream.

With a dash of sprinkles, she hands me the fanciest coffee ever. It's similar to the one she made me yesterday, but something about this one feels different.

We walk toward the living room where the bay window blinds are open. Upon inspection, I realize it's not simply white outside, we're snowed in.

Setting down my coffee, I go to the window, noticing the snow is all the way to about two inches from the top of the window.

"Holy shit," I mutter. "There are no snowmen to be made."

She comes to my side, resting her head on my chest. It's almost like it's natural for her, so I widen my stance, wrapping my arm around her.

I'm supposed to be her teacher, but it seems like she's learning all these things naturally. The thought of someone experiencing them with her isn't something I'm too fond of.

"Guess Mother Nature is going to kick my ass this time."

"This time?" I chuckle, wondering what she's talking about. She nods against my chest.

"I wanted snow, to be festive last night, and I made it."

"You can change the weather?" This is news to me, good news, crazy news, holy crap. She smiles and nods.

"As Cupids, we sometimes need to manipulate it slightly. We don't control it much, just start a snow storm or a rain one. We can warm areas and bring winds. The control is out of our hands, though."

"Which brings this snowed-in cottage."

"Exactly," she admits.

I kiss the top of her head before thinking better of it. "Sounds like a movie day."

She jumps from my side with a pleased expression. "I get to bore you with questions all day?"

"Yes," I confirm, humor making my smile massive. "But as soon as night comes, you're mine and we're doing our next lesson."

Heat flashes in her expression and she must know it'll be more than kissing. We only have four days left. By Christmas, I'll be gone and she'll be with the love of her life.

Either way, she has a lot to learn, and I hope I'm the only one who will teach her. There's a selfish part of me that longs to be that love.

Then again, that's not what we agreed on.

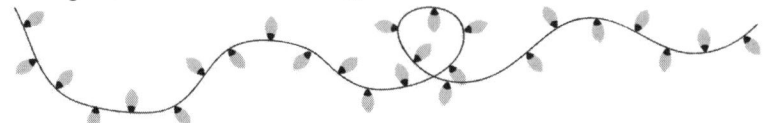

She asks me so many questions. If my dad looks like Santa; if I'm a redhead and dye my hair dark. Technically, my hair is so dark it appears black, but yes, it's red. The darkest shade known to man, that is.

"I think the sun is setting," I say to her hours later, after we've had a marathon of cheesy Christmas rom-coms and Hallmark movies. She pointed out the love she sought. The fake store-bought kind that isn't what she deserves.

She'll learn soon enough.

The bar isn't on the floor, it's so high that they better fly over the fucking bar before I accept them as her possible mate.

"How can you tell?" she questions.

"The clock says six at night, Joyful. Which means, the fun's over, and it's my turn to teach."

She blinks at me slowly. "W-what's on tonight's lesson plan, Professor Claus?" Fuck, the way the words come out quiet and lax, like she barely breathed while reciting them, gets me instantly hard.

I stand and she follows, a part of me wishes she has lingerie. It would be an excellent step for this plan.

"Do you have lace?" I request, knowing that the thought of fucking her is too big for me to handle. She'll have to touch herself tonight. *Without* my assisting hands.

Her eyes seem to soften, almost melting, as if she's thought of this. She nods, slow, like she needs me to see it.

"Go get changed," I direct, pointing at her room. She takes no time to walk away, rushing to do as I say. A part of me assumed she'd be shy.

Her brazenness has come full force in the last three nights. She's proud and she knows she's sexy. I'm not sure when that changed, but I can't wait to watch her blossom and fall apart before my eyes.

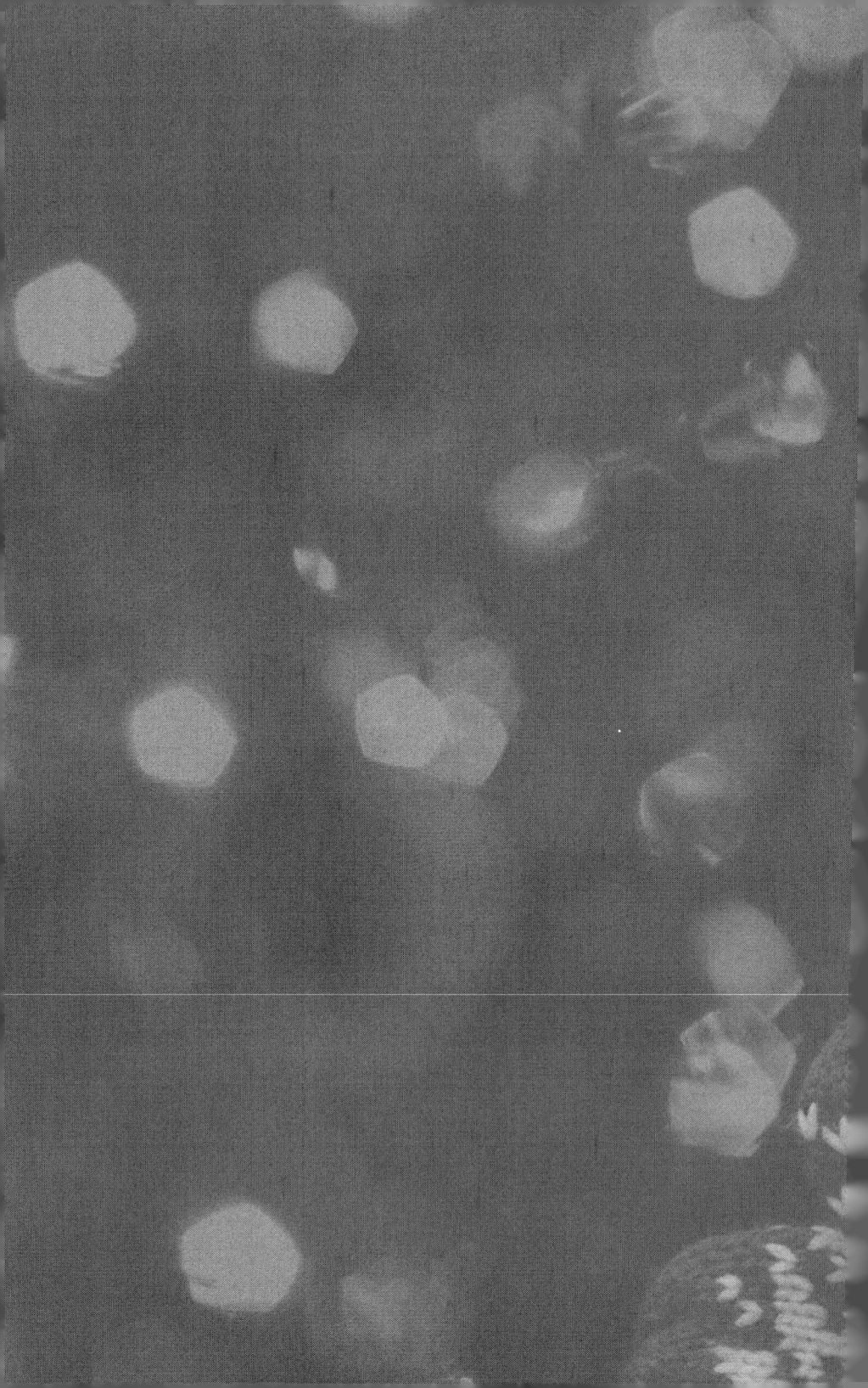

## CHAPTER 15

### SANTA BABY — EARTHA KITT

### XO

**M**y body shakes as my eyes connect with the ensemble I bought last week. It was a random purchase. At the mall, before Santa came, I stopped at a shop. Browsing all the frilly things, I knew I wanted to experience it firsthand.

When braving the inside, this red and white striped lingerie set caught my attention. It's strappy, wrapping around me like a present.

Attached is a garter, and it latches onto my stockings.

I've never worn something like this, and I'm so grateful I went against my apprehension and purchased it. Now, it's here. It'll show Arson I'm ready for love, that I'm capable of being sexy.

I wish my brain would catch the memo. My hands hover over the material and I still shudder. Fear and excitement dance in tandem together, keeping me from putting it on and also enticing me to wear it.

Would he fall to his knees? Will he think I'm sensual?

I take a deep breath and shuck off my clothes. Hurrying with all the straps, I put it on and let out the most anxious sigh.

Part of me wants to go right out to him, strut, make him see *me*. The other—the one who is still a damn virgin who wants sex—she leads me to the bathroom.

As soon as I meet my reflection, I wheeze. It's nearly silent, but still there. I'm flushed, but not in a way that makes me seem shy. It's the kind I've read about. The type that's expectant from pleasure.

The blown pupils, heated skin, and feeling of prickling needles across my body. I look incredible, from head to toe.

He's going to die.

A smirk frees itself from my uneasy mind. Decidedly, I grab a robe and then head to him. I'm not thinking twice.

He wants me. This will prove it.

Walking out of my room, I note his turned frame. His shirt is gone and the breadth of his wingspan meets me. Shit, he's so powerful in this stance. His thighs are thick, only covered halfway. Where his boxer briefs cover.

He either felt my presence or noticed my loud intake of breath, either way he turns to me, and I stumble.

Catching myself on the railing near the bottom of the stairs, I place a hand on my chest. "Shit."

His eyes go from my toes to my eyes, so slowly, I swear I aged a decade in his pursuit. Heat dances in his eyes, molten.

I rub my neck for comfort, for confidence, and he folds his arms across his chest. "Take it off." It's a command. Not cruel, but expectant.

He's devouring me without words and knowing I have that power at all has a wetness pooling between my thighs.

Foreign. Wet. What is this?

I reach for the sash, pulling the tie. With a little shrug, the silky material falls to the floor and Arson immediately notices.

"Fuck, Joyful. This should be goddamn illegal to witness."

Without guidance, I twirl, making sure it's slow and purposeful. His eyes haven't left me, but they eventually make it to my own.

"Like?"

"Like?" he hisses, his voice deep and desperate. "Any person would be fucking dumb not to be obsessed."

"Are you?" I prod, seeing the tent in his briefs. He's so hard that I know he'll be wrecking my insides at some point.

That's where this leads to, right?

To a place where he fucks me and I cry from pleasure?

Heat, wetness, and desire as lethal as the volcanoes in Darchon meets between my thighs, promising so much.

I've never experienced these sensations. They're different and welcome. And I wonder if it's sticky or more liquid like water?

It's a reaction to being aroused, I'm not stupid. However, I'm just not one hundred percent sure on how my own anatomy works.

"Don't just stand there," he growls, the gentlemanly stance he usually has disappears. Arson sits on the couch, similar to a place from when I spilled my coffee. "Tell Santa what you want, Joyful."

This time, instead of being anxious about what I want and how I want it, I'll tell him exactly what I crave. Whether or not it's how it works is not my problem. There's a throb and ache between my legs and somehow, I know he'll assuage it.

"Please," I whimper. He taps his lap once more, his gaze darkening as he bites his fist.

"Come here."

I don't make him tell me twice, I practically skip the distance to his lap. "Yes, Santa."

He sits back, his legs wide, the tenting of his bottoms have me wondering what's beneath them. His eyes haven't left mine. We're both entranced by the other.

I place my thighs around his, not sitting on him like I have the last two times. This time, we're face to face, our bodies flush.

If he's shocked, he doesn't show it. All I can see is red, toned abs, and a face full of promise.

"Such a good girl, listening to me without argument."

I happily nod, warmth spreading down to my toes. As if he notices how wet the fabric between my thighs is, he bites his lip and adjusts me. His erection presses upward and I sit directly in front of it.

Up close, it's even more daunting. It's like a weapon.

"Scared?"

I nod once. "I know what I want for Christmas, Santa."

Approval paints his features, mixed with hope. His eyebrows are drawn in as I wiggle to situate myself better.

"What do you want, Joyful?" His voice is pure gravel, like he's grinding rocks with his molars to sound so wrecked.

"I want to feel good, Santa," I explain, moving on top of him again. This time, I feel pleasure zip up my spine as I rub directly against him.

He lets out a sharp hiss. His gaze zeroes in on the material barely covering my pussy. Almost like he's wanting to evaporate it, slide right inside after.

"How do you want to feel good?" he prods, wanting more words. Better descriptors.

"An orgasm," I squeak, gulping back my mortification. That word has never been shameful to say aloud, but sitting on the lap of a monster whose cock presses against me aggressively, makes me a little insecure. He's gorgeous. Muscular, big, and so gorgeous.

His finger and thumb tilt my chin upward. "Look right here."

Our gazes connect, and the molten lust he shows me has a little whimper escaping me. "Please touch my pussy."

"Mmm," he approves, his cock twitching in response. "I love when you tell me what you want."

"Please touch me, Santa. I've been good all year." As if those words spur him on, he leans back and gestures to his dick.

"Use me. Rub your pretty little cunt on me until you come. Show me how you like to get off."

"But I—" I begin to make an excuse, about how I've never touched myself, but he stops me. His thumb hovers over my lace-covered clit, and he barely presses down.

I nearly jump as desire violently zips through me. "See, Joyful. You know what feels good, now make yourself come on my cock so we can both learn."

# CHAPTER 16

## CHRISTMAS EVE — JUSTIN BIEBER

# ARSON

Her nervousness is too attractive, it draws me in. I wasn't even going to allow her to rub off on me. Hell, I planned on staying clothed. But then I wanted her to see what she does to me. To men in general. I needed her to know she's the hottest fucking woman I've ever met, and she'd see it visually. She deserves to be desired and shown that she's drop-dead fucking sexy.

She doesn't take too long before she gently rocks against my cock. The veins in my head feel so near combustion as I hold back my control. Her wetness leaks through the lace, it's drenching the fabric of my boxer briefs.

I bet if she moved, she'd see it. Does she taste sweet? I'd devour her whole. Lick her from clit to asshole and make sure she screamed my name.

Fuck.

The things I want to teach her. *If only we had time.*

"Am I doing this right?" she breathily questions, her chest rising and falling in rapid succession. She's pressing against me, her thick thighs gripping mine for leverage. She moves slowly, gently, like she's too scared of the sensations.

"Rock harder, sweetness. Press your clit against me like you'll die if you don't find your release."

The words spur her on, her entire body shuddering as she rides my lap. Her ass presses against my thighs, and while I said I wouldn't touch her, I can't resist but to grip it. Her cheeks are thick, so fucking graspable. Two handfuls that help her press harder against me.

"Yes, Arson, right there," she encourages me. I help her. Against my best fucking judgement, I assist her hips. She shudders with every undulation. Her entire body's a shaking mess above me.

She's so close, I can tell with the way her lips draws up in a pleasure-filled O.

The realization that she'll come on my cock has me nervous. Will she regret this afterward?

"You're such a good girl, Joyful. Look at you riding my cock like it's yours." She pants and releases a low moan. It's deep and dragged out from her, building up, much like her release. "Let it out, sweetness. Come for me."

"Arson," she whimpers. "It feels so good."

"It'll feel even better when you let go. You can do this," I assure her, grinding her hips in tandem with my own. We're a rutting mess of shaking legs and throbbing limbs. My cock specifically, it's also ready.

"If you come for me, I'll come with you," I promise, feeling my balls tighten. Her eyes open and our gazes collide.

She expels out the loudest cry. "Arson, please!" I can feel my cock pulse. The buildup is too much, and as her body shakes, her orgasm overcoming her, my own rushes from me.

"Fuck, Joyful," I hiss her nickname, loving the way she keeps her pace, chasing her high. My cock twitches twice more before it releases. And fuck, my entire body feels wrecked.

I've never had an orgasm like this. I've seen it in amateur porn, but never experienced it with anyone.

My entire body feels like it's on fire, which is saying something since I'm a draegyn. Her eyes roam my body appreciatively, while sweat lines her brow.

"Did I do it right?" she asks, her chest still heaving from her orgasm. She's perfect like this, exerted, free, and soft.

My cock is still hard, ready for more, and as if she notices, she stares. "I must've done it wrong, you're still stiff."

I try not to smirk, knowing it's just because I'm a constant masochist. "You did it perfectly," I soothe, my hands still cupping her ass.

She points at me. "Then why are you like that?" Renewed anxiety shines in her eyes.

"I'm solid because all I want to do is sink inside you," I grittily confess, adjusting my erection. Grabbing her hand, I place it over the obvious wet spot. "Like you, I had a mind-blowing orgasm."

Her hand flexes over my head, her fingers trailing down my body. "I want to see you."

I shake my head immediately, knowing her lesson is done. "You aced your lesson. It's time for something else."

"You said all night," she parries, her eyebrows raising, calling me out on my bullshit. "It's only seven."

She adjusts on me, reaching for the waistband of my boxer briefs. "This is about you," I deflect, flipping us so she's on the couch and I'm hovering above her.

"You don't think I'll need to know how to please my lover?" The way her innocent mouth says lover wrecks me.

"That's not—"

"You're teaching me how to find love, Arson. Show me how to please the one I'll love."

"Fuck," I echo my earlier thoughts. "Tomorrow." I'm trying so hard to set limits here. We're getting in too deep, and far too quickly. I need her to have some restraint too.

Once we hit a certain point, walking away will destroy us both. We're not in this for the long haul. Even if my heart has other ideas.

"Please," she requests, her hand slides up my chest like she knows every ridge. Maybe she does. Maybe like me, she only has two speeds. Dreaming of sex and testing out limits. I'm too desperate to escape my own fantasies and instead, I nod.

"First, I want to show you what any lover should do. If they don't, they're not the fucking one."

Her eyes twinkle with playfulness. She knows she's won this round of our battle of wills. And fuck if that doesn't make me want her more.

Spreading her thighs, the fabric between them hugs her slit. It sits right above it, tight, like it needs to be gone. It's like a big candy cane, stretched and wrapped around her perfectly.

"You're perfect," I admire, my hands still lingering on her spread legs.

I want to slide them up her, part her, and eat her out. Her moans will be fucking beautiful. But I also want to relish this.

"What are you supposed to show me?" she questions, as my eyes don't leave her cunt, imaging all the things I plan to do.

"I'm just memorizing this," I grunt, feeling harder than moments before when she touched my cock.

She bites her lip, her brow furrowing with concern. I forget she doesn't know me, doesn't know what I look like when I'm near combustion, or when I'm losing all sense of control. I'm fucking ravenous.

"I know you've never kissed or had an orgasm," I rasp, feeling my control wash away with all the promises I silently made myself about not falling too deep. "But have you been touched..." I slide my hand up her thigh, pausing where it meets her pussy. "Here?"

She lets out a sharp intake of breath, her eyes blown out with arousal. Yeah, she likes this spot.

"N-no," she whimpers. I trail closer, putting more pressure. The contrast between my deep red skin and her bubblegum pink thighs could be an art form.

"What about here?" I ask, my finger outlining her cunt with intention. She bites her lip hard and I want to take it between my own teeth. She doesn't answer with words. Instead, she shakes her head softly. "And here?" I growl, unable to control the feral way I'm mapping her body for my own undoing.

She pushes toward my fingers tracing her below the lace. She whines when my finger brushes her clit.

This time she nods.

Shock, violent and red, hits me. "What?"

"Earlier, you pressed against it when teaching me." A smirk with full mischief covers her face and she giggles when my shoulders relax.

"You're a little monster, you know that?"

She smiles, her teeth fully showing. It's good to see this part of her. The soft side that loves to make you happy.

I tug at the lace covering her until it rips. Her eyes widen, and unlike what I expected, she doesn't complain about ruining them.

Leaning forward, I kiss the inside of her knee, leading all the way to her cunt. With a deep inhale, my brain nearly frazzles with how sweet she smells. A deep-rooted moan escapes her throat when I drag my nose along her slit and press it against her clit.

"Arson," she implores. Too consumed with my need to taste her, I don't even look to see what she's begging for. I slide my hands up to her pussy, spreading her apart, and flatten my tongue against her sex. "Oh my goddess."

She writhes above me, her eyes full of arousal and desperation. One that matches my own. I take no time, licking up her slowly, tracing her clit with purpose. Circle after circle, I tease, and fuck, she tastes mouthwatering.

She's as sweet as I expected.

"More," she pleads, her head falling backward with the request. Rising higher on my knees, I dip my finger around her entrance, gathering her dripping arousal. It's sticky and so fucking hot.

Her eyes stay closed as I hover. "Open your mouth," I direct, pressing my finger to her closed lips. She drops them open, her eyes following suit. "Taste how delicious you are."

She nods as I press my wet digit into her mouth. Tentatively, her tongue darts out, swirling around my finger.

There's no way she realizes how fucking sexy she is, and how good she looks with her flushed face, blown eyes, and swollen lips begging for my own.

"When you're with the man you want to please, he needs to return the favor. If he doesn't lick your cunt and make you squirt, he's not the one," I remind her, my desire for her doubling as she nods and wraps her mouth around my finger entirely, sucking it deeper.

My thoughts overpower me, imagining her mouth around my cock, sucking it down with uncertainty. She'd probably play with it, lick it like a sucker.

Shit.

I pull out from her mouth, the resounding pop surprising us both. Fervor burns inside me as I lean forward and lick her lip, making sure there's nothing left.

"I like this lesson," she praises me. I take no time to drop back down.

"Not over yet, Joyful. Not until you cry out my name."

Her throat moves as she swallows, and that's where I'll be next. Nipping her skin. Not breaking it, though—she's not mine to claim.

# CHAPTER 17

ALL I WANT FOR CHRISTMAS IS YOU – MARIAH CAREY

## XO

He's perfect.

I never thought this was how it would go when I asked Santa to find me love. This is so much more than a Cupid does. We snap our fingers and it's done. One and done, not too much push and pull.

But as Arson kneels between my thighs, his tongue flicking my clit with practiced stokes, I realize I have no freaking clue what love is.

Because if love is the way I fall apart to his tongue on me, and that overwhelming building of ardor between my thighs, I'm a goner for this monster.

If it's deeper, like how he looks at me, how I feel when he smirks... then I was gone the day we met, and that thought scares me even more.

Too frazzled with possibilities, I'm shocked silly when his tongue breaches my hole. "Shit!" I yell out, realizing I don't curse often, let alone out loud in his presence. He pulls back and worry creases his forehead.

"I'm okay," I reassure. "It just feels... overwhelming." And it does. It feels like I'm winning the lottery or having blueberry pie for the first time.

It's a tangible experience that has no proper description other than I want to feel it repeatedly.

He leans forward once more. "Relax."

I do, taking a deep breath. Pleasure zips up my spine when he does it again. "Right there," I encourage, thinking about earlier when he helped me get off on his lap.

He's so big, and when he gripped me and helped me thrust against him, I thought I'd perish from how good it felt.

His tongue penetrates me over and over, and I find tears forming as my entire body floats with euphoric pleasure.

"Please let me come," I whimper as wetness pools from me. He growls, nipping my clit, and then he licks and teases my entrance with his finger. The ridges of his tongue that I felt when we kissed press against me.

"Since you said please," he answers as he continues his work. I bow off the couch and he uses his other hand to press me into it more. His ministrations don't stop and the lightest feeling overwhelms my brain. The movement, the heat, and the tingles overwhelm me.

As soon as his lips wrap around my bundle of nerves, I'm a goner, my legs shake as he works me through my orgasm.

"Arson!" I scream out his name while falling apart. My body feels like absolute jelly, but the pleasure hasn't stopped throbbing between my thighs.

He traces the freckles on my thighs with his fingers, and I note his eyes are dark. Ravenous. I want to please him, show him I want his pleasure too.

I'm not entirely sure how to do that, but maybe he'll teach me. I want to learn.

"Your turn," I whisper, my voice strained from how wrecked I feel. My eyes seem to weigh down. Heavier with each breath.

My Monster Claus smirks at me, leaving a chaste kiss atop my pussy before he lifts me. His steps are silent as he carries me to the bedroom. Sudden tiredness has me shivering and he must notice since the heat of his body increases.

"Where are you taking me?" I whisper, feeling absolutely exhausted. I've never felt this kind of weariness. Especially so random and swift.

"Bathroom?"

"Over there," I attempt to point but my arm falls. "Why do I feel so fatigued?" The words come out slurred as I attempt to speak them.

"Sometimes pleasure brings a lot of dopamine, so we're going to warm you up and clean you off."

I don't know if I nod or not, but he sets me down in the tub, slowly removing my lingerie. It's not sexual in any way, and somehow, that's super comforting to me. He turns on the water, warming it up. Not too hot, not too cool.

"I like this," I ramble, feeling like I'm speaking in cursive. He presses a kiss to my forehead, and I sigh happily.

"What do you need, Joyful?"

Need? "What do you mean?"

"Do you need me to rub your back, massage your body, or even clean you? I want to take care of you."

Emotion clogs my mind, tears pricking at the edges of my eyes. Being starved for affection your entire life will do that to you.

"Hold me," I whimper, silently weeping. He takes no time to climb in behind me, holding me. Forming a cup, he lifts water, trailing it down my back.

He's so gentle as he holds me to him, slowly warming me up. His fingers never linger inappropriately, and he continues to lather my back and arms.

When he reaches my chest, soapy hands moving, I mold his hands over my breasts. There's a part of me that wants to sink into his skin and stay there forever. The most I can do is force our bodies closer by using his own as my leverage.

As if he gets the idea, he pulls my back flush to his front. "I've got you,

Xóchitl," he rasps, reassuring me. He hardly uses my name, especially not my full one. It seems more intimate somehow, like he needs me to know this is him and me.

Not his Joyful. Not my monster.

Just us.

We stay like this, pressed against each other, a type of comfort I've never experienced. He continues to heat the water with his body changing temperatures, and I just melt into him. Whether or not he realizes it, he's the best hugger. His arms wrap around my shoulders now, boxing me in.

I've never felt safer than this moment.

"Can I wash your hair?" he asks. It's gentle, not pushy at all. He knows I'm not a fan of having it touched. It's very curly. It has to be treated well. Not only that, the process of taking care of curly hair isn't easy. It's time-consuming and requires a type of love and tenderness not everyone has the patience for.

But yet, I nod.

He leans forward, kissing my shoulder. I'm not even sure if he notices that he pursues any reason to touch me.

I do it too.

Whether it's holding his hand or waist, I seek him out. Then the other half of time, I'm hoping he reaches for me, touches me, and I'm not sure what to think about that.

Arson stands, reaching up for my shampoo, conditioner, and oils. He takes his time wetting my hair. He massages my scalp, his hands gentle and purposeful.

There's nothing quite like having every inch of you cared for by another, and this is by far the most intimate I've been with someone.

If it were anyone but Arson, I couldn't do this. I just know it.

What scares me is that it's days before Christmas and he'll be leaving me soon. Then I'll be with someone else. That's the deal... right?

Why does acknowledging that have dread consuming me?

MAEVE BLACK

# CHAPTER 18

## WHITE CHRISTMAS — ONEREPUBLIC

## ARSON

After I finish her hair, she passes out. Throughout the night, I never let her go.

Right now, I'm pressed against her headboard, her body snuggled against me as I draw snowman shapes on her back.

I've never been this close to a woman.

I'm not really one for more than sex, but even then, I don't do that often either. She's holding on to me like I'm her lifeline, and she's teaching me that there's more to life than duty.

We've decorated, gone through lights in the park, and now all I can think about is making her smile more.

She has the perfect one too. Her dimples only peek through with mischief and pure glee. I'm going to make it my goal to do that for her, make her happy.

I barely slept through the night. Day's breaking through and the snow still stands overwhelmingly high. It melted a little, but it's covers most everything. The news station said there's going to be a national snow week at this rate. They'll let us know as time proceeds. The plows can't even un-bury themselves.

It's okay, though, being this close to Xó. Doing whatever she wants is enough for me. And that is a terrifying thought.

I could stay here.

Run away with her and experience life.

It's too damn tempting and that freaks me out. We're only here for another four days. That's too short to think about longer.

We both have responsibilities.

I'm Santa, she's Cupid, yet all I want is her.

Movement catches my attention, and when I peer down, she's staring at me. There's an emotion present, but I can't quite decipher it.

"Good morning."

She stretches a little, yawning while I hold her close. It's unintentional, natural even. Letting go of her seems too fucking gloomy.

"Morning," she sleepily responds, sitting up. Untangled, she attempts to stand, but I tug her arm, bringing our faces together.

Unsure of what brought me to kissing her freely, I don't question it. I just devour her mouth and fall into her as she gives back.

Once she's gasping for air, she lets out a happy sigh. "Coffee?"

"You're going to get me addicted to something I've never had before," I protest, thinking of many other things I'm unused to and am slowly becoming desperate for.

She heads out to the kitchen, and I struggle to find how to deflate my already hard dick.

It would take a lot, but I know just the cure. Heading to the other room, I grab my phone from my bag, calling Pyro.

"Going to let me in on when you're coming back? Time's running short."

"Later. Have a question, though."

In the background, a door closes, and I'm sure he's taking himself away from prying ears. A chair scooting out is the last sound I hear before he replies. "Shoot."

"What do you know of Cupids?"

"Cupids? Like the old fable of finding true love by being shot with an arrow?" I don't laugh and that alone tells him I'm not joking. "I know little about them."

Something in his tone seems like it's untrue. "Why don't I believe you?" The words are accusatory. It's easy to know when a sibling lies after knowing them for many centuries. My brother is no different.

"Okay, but you've got to keep tight-lipped." Not offering him a response, I wait for his explanation. "Shit, okay. So, I fucked around with one once."

"And?"

"He was probably the best lay I've ever had."

I audibly groan. "Seriously? That's all you've got?"

He lets out these silent mocking noises, and I know I've somehow hit a nerve. "Cupids have rules. It's forbidden to find love or want for more than reproduction, and whatnot."

"What kind of barbaric shit is that?" I complain, thinking of how innocent Xó is. It's no wonder she doesn't have a clue about what feels good until it does.

"I know," he agrees, his voice aggressive like he has a bone to pick with their goddess. "He and I found each other randomly. It was good, dude. Felt like I was constantly high on him."

"Shit," I mutter under my breath, thinking of where my mind went. That's exactly what I want to know. "Do you know if they have special drug-inducing qualities?"

More noises sound out at my ear before glass moving tells me he's getting a glass of the good stuff. "No clue," he responds. Nothing in his inflection says he's lying this time. "Why do you ask?"

"No reason." I shut his question down immediately. He can't know I'm fucking around with one and I can't be falling for her either.

"Well, that's a stupid reason to call," he complains, his irritation apparent. "Don't be dipping your candy cane in a Cupid, Arson. They can't—"

"Arson?" Xó's voice sounds out. I hang up on Pyro and pretend I'm getting a change of clothes. It's not inaccurate, I do in fact need to wear something. But I also look distrustful as hell when I turn around to her.

"Hey," I reply, wishing the rampant heartbeat echoing in my head would settle. She looks so cute with her mug of coffee and an extra one for me. "What's on the agenda today?"

Suspicion paints her features briefly before she hands me the mug. I take it and hide behind it as I drink.

"Gingerbread houses," she finally answers, as if asking me what I was up to just now will ruin the mood. It would. There's no doubt she'd hate me for ever questioning if her intentions were good and if she's somehow mindlessly affecting me.

Part of the doubt creeps in. What if she doesn't like me back? It would easily be explained as pheromones. I'm consumed by her, at an addictive rate, but she seems fine.

"I've never made those," I admit. One thing we don't take much part in at the North Pole is baking. We do fun things, but that's not one of them.

My mind travels to the drakes. To the way they're basically little kids at heart. It's been so long since I've spent time with them, making sure they're happy.

"What!" her exclamation catches me off guard. She puts a hand on my chest, blinking and laughing. "I'm sorry, I just haven't met anyone who hasn't made them before. Not someone with your Santa-like origin, at least."

"How many red suit men do you know?" I tease, and she sticks out her tongue.

"Only you," she chastises. "But as Santa, you should have all these experiences at least once. It's crazy that you've never made gingerbread houses.

Isn't that like Christmas 101?"

"There's no handbook, Joyful. We don't play by the rules."

The expression of pure heat on her face has me nearly taking her mouth with mine, but fuck, I need to stop doing that. We didn't set up boundaries when this started. We didn't have rules.

How the hell am I going to leave her?

"So, gingerbread?" I break the tension, knowing I can't stay here for much longer. She's too tempting, and I'm too wrecked.

After she gathers all the supplies between her pantry and the fridge, I wait for her guidance. She wraps an apron around her waist, it's green with frilly edges and little cottages all over the fabric. I smile at the way she twirls with it, the uncanny joy she brings to every moment of our day motivates me to love Christmas and appreciate the small things.

"I bought these cut-outs and since the dough will need to sit, I figured we could do the easy part. Right now, the dough is our primary focus," she explains, pointing at the house shapes.

It's cute seeing her so serious about something, and I love the fact that she's dedicated to Christmas like it's her entire livelihood.

She grabs the butter she had let sit out. It's soft in appearance, and she unwraps it. Placing it in a bowl, she grabs some weird brown liquid. My guess is it's what gives the cookies the coloring.

"I'm going to beat the butter until it's creamy, and then add the sugar and molasses," she explains, all while my mind sticks on her words that could be read out of context as innuendos.

"What do I do?" I laugh, watching her dive right into the bowl with a mixing instrument. She rolls her eyes playfully.

"Stand and look cute, because I'll need you to knead the dough later. Save your strength because I'm making you do all the work."

I scoot closer to her, standing behind her but at an angle. Unable to help myself, I place my hands on her waist, loving how they fit perfectly there.

She rotates as she mixes, and it's a different side of her I've yet to experience. One I can say I absolutely adore.

After she adds in all the spices, she continues mixing everything by hand. Almost like it's necessary for the manual movement over quick ones.

I don't know how much time passes as we do this, but she stops and covers the bowl.

"What now?"

"This has to chill for about three to four hours."

"Then what?"

She throws me a warning glare. "You knead the dough, and we bake them." Tilted, she puts her arms around my shoulders. It's so intimate and personal, and we do it so naturally. Is this her way of being taught?

Naturally observant and fucking phenomenal at it?

"Now?"

She stands on her tiptoes, leaning in. Her breath fans against my throat while I hold my breath. "Now, you teach me how to bring you pleasure."

Fuck.

## CHAPTER 19

SLEIGH RIDE – THE RONETTES

XO

He stares at me wide-eyed, and the fact that I caught him off guard is so satisfying.

There's a nagging feeling at the back of my mind of how evasive he was earlier. It seemed like he was speaking to someone, but the hushed tones didn't give me anything. By the time I mustered the courage to ask him what was up, he shut down.

I haven't seen him look that nervous since he allowed me to get off on him yesterday. It was a similar fear, something along the lines of not knowing what he's feeling.

I shake that off, though. Desire flows through me as a result of wanting to taste him like he did me. Last night, after he took care of me and my hair, I dreamed of him. Of how he tasted, and how I wanted to bring him the same kind of bliss.

If he melts under my tongue like I did for him, it would make me happy. He's an excellent teacher—too good, to be quite honest.

There are moments where I wonder if he's educating or simply experiencing, and I get confused. My heart beats faster when he looks at me in a specific way. Similar to now.

There's intrigue in his green eyes, almost an uncanny desperation that matches mine. But it has to be for show, I'm sure of it. We agreed to a trade-off, but I didn't realize we'd both end with us getting off on one another.

"Don't you want to do other things?" he asks, and for the first time since meeting him, my monster seems... *nervous*.

Deciding to take the lead, I grab his wrist, heading toward my bedroom. Before I can hit the hallway, he stops me, pivoting toward the living room.

A part of me wonders if that's how he keeps it less personal. More like lessons and less like romance.

Is that what this is, romance?

"How do you want to do this?"

For once, we don't start with me in his lap, him forcing me to tell him what I want. This time, he wants me to lead. I'm not entirely sure how to do that.

"How do you like to be touched?" I whisper, nerves crawling through my veins like little spider legs. This is usually his role here, not mine. He leads and I follow. Maybe more like melt into a puddle, but generally, he's the teacher.

His little devious smirk tilts at his lips and I'm obsessed with the way it sends shivers across my body.

"Any way you touch me, I'll like that."

"That's a cop-out," I protest, pushing him down on the couch. He falls in a heap, spreading his thighs with the confidence of a man who knows what gets him off.

"That's what I like, watching you explore me like I'm yours to unwrap." He says the words so matter of fact that I'm at a loss. My jaw flies open, and he uses his forefinger to close it.

The couch has always been a charming and ugly thing, but right now, I can't think of a better piece of furniture. Sliding down to my knees, I exhale. Something about having total control both scares and entices me.

He will let me touch him this time.

Bare.

I lick my lips, my gaze falling to his lap. It's already tented with his arousal. Do I turn him on?

Sitting on the back of my heels, I wonder where to start. If I watched porn, I'd be far more versed, but I don't know what to do.

Sure, I can deduce what I enjoy, but how do I know what will make him lose his mind?

"Take off my pants," he guides when I'm stuck in my brain. His voice is smoky, like he's barely holding back, and that spurs me on.

My hands fumble on his button, but as soon as that's undone and I'm pulling on his zipper, excitement has my nerves leaving.

He's letting me touch him.

He's allowing me to go for it.

I open his jeans, pulling on his waistband. Yesterday, he stopped me from going further. Right now, as I look up at him through my lashes, he's not holding me back. He wants this.

Placing my fingers beneath the band, I inch forward and am in shock. Just the root of him is so thick. My fingers can't touch and when I try to wrap them around him, I simply can't.

He says nothing as I explore him. He's still hidden beneath his boxer briefs, and it's enticing to be cut off visually.

When I drag my nails down across his balls, he lets out a guttural groan. It's so deep and restrained. Our gazes meet, his appears sedated. His lids are half closed and his jaw is tight, ticking as his nostrils flare.

We say nothing as I tease his length with featherlight touches. With no guidance, I stumble a little, but he gives me his fangs, which are now longer than they were last night. It urges me on, telling me he's enjoying this torment. Even if only a little.

Unwilling to waste more time, I pull his boxers down. Sprung free, his cock is impressive. And holy shit. It's candy cane colored.

"Is this real?" I hesitate while asking. From his balls to his tip, he's red and white striped like a candy cane.

He smiles wickedly, his fangs spilling outside his top lip. "Where do you think they got the idea of sucking on candy canes from?" he taunts, grabbing my hand and placing it on his length. Before my eyes, it curves, just like a candy cane.

I lick my lips, wondering how it would taste.

"Do it," he encourages, his cock still curved. I start low, licking upward with enthusiasm. He tastes sweet, and there are a few things I love more than sugar. His ragged groan vibrates his body, almost as if he's growling from deep within. When I get to the curved portion, I do what I do to candy canes, take the entire hook—or attempt to—into my mouth.

His hand immediately finds my hair, gripping it with praise. "Fuck, Xó," he huskily moans my name and I sigh around the part of him inside my mouth.

He massages my head, helping me around his hook. Too enamored, I suck his entire tip into my mouth, savoring the addicting flavor.

As my mouth is still wrapped around him, he shifts it straight. It assists me taking him deeper. He's massive, though, and while I'm messily sucking every available inch I can, I'm not the best at it.

I can't believe he has a fucking candy cane cock.

MAEVE BLACK

## CHAPTER 20

### THE CHRISTMAS SONG – NAT KING COLE

## ARSON

There aren't many things I can say with all honesty that rock my world. But seeing my doe-eyed Cupid on her knees, licking my cock like it's her favorite treat, might be at the top of the list.

Drool pools at the edges of her lips, and it's hard to not just lick it from her. She's doing so well. Her curly head bobs up and down, gagging, but pushing further and further. It's addictive as fuck.

My only craving is the wetness between her thighs. I imagine when our cum mixes, it'll taste like a peppermint cookie.

The thought has me yearning for things I can't have. We never agreed to sex, not that it's off the table—not for me, at least.

"You're taking me so well," I praise, my words coming out broken and breathless. She's wrecking me. I'm fucking undone by her mouth and nervous hands stroking me.

Her attention flies to me, and the glazed-over look is too much. It's too much for me to hold back anymore.

"How far will you go, Xóchitl? How much do you want to learn?"

Her eyes narrow as she continues her ministrations, and that tells me too fucking much. "Your words, Xóchitl. I need your fucking words."

She pops off me and her drool slides down her face. She licks her cock-swollen lips, her eyes devouring me. I drag my thumb over her wet chin, wiping her mess away.

"I want you to be my first," she admits, her signature flush painting her cheeks and chest. My body seems to freeze at her words. Did she just say that?

It's been a replaying thought since showing up here, but most of that was my dick speaking. The logical part of me didn't think it was a realistic thought.

"Take it," I lowly command, overwhelmed with all my fantasies coming to fruition.

"How will I know what to do if you don't show me first?"

Those words immediately deflate me, popping the thought that this was more. It reminds me of my place. I'm teaching her. Showing her how to please her lover.

That's all.

"Riding me will be the least painful," I explain, not diving into the feelings festering behind my rib cage. "You'll be able to control how much you take."

Our gazes lock and she seems to ponder what I've offered. "I can take all of you," she finally says and that throbbing inside my balls intensifies. Does she not realize how fucking sexy it is when she says shit like that? "I want you to fuck me like you would if I were any other person."

"Fuck, Joyful. You can't say shit like that," I confess, the drunk feeling overwhelming every sense. Her tongue flicks out to tease my tip again, slow and sure.

"I'm your present tonight, Santa. That's what I want. For you to unwrap me and use me." She punctuates her words with little nips across my cockhead.

"Lay back, close your eyes," I softly instruct. She goes to the back of her heels and rolls onto her back. Without direction, she spreads her thighs. Even fully dressed, she's irresistible. "Eyes closed." They shut, no argument.

I rush to her box of Christmas decorations in the closet. After decorating the tree, we watched movies while we adorned the entire house. And now, with what's left, I put my fantasies to the test.

Grabbing what I need, my cock throbs. I take no time to rid myself of my pants, boxer briefs, and shirt. I unfurl my wings, freeing them, needing them to be a part of this.

When I come back, the little minx freed herself of her clothes too. "You little monster," I chastise. She covers her eyes, her fingers splitting when I come over. "No peeking!"

She giggles, but I'm sure she saw everything stuffed in my arms. Beneath me, she's naked. Her legs shut this time, and I know that has more to do with teasing me than being modest.

I set down the ribbon, ornaments, and string lights I stole from her stash. She's going to be a perfect little tree. I'll wrap her like a present and fuck her like she's mine.

"Hiding, are we?" I tease, tracing a finger down her bare thigh. She wiggles, little blotches of goosebumps flaring all over her skin.

She splits her thighs, showing me what I've been craving since I tasted her last night. Her orgasm wasn't enough. I simply need more.

"I need you to pick a word, one where you can use it and I'll stop. So I never hurt you or overstep your boundaries."

She uncovers her eyes, but only peers into mine, her gaze not searching what items are nearby. "Cocoa?"

I smile, thinking of how much she seems to love sweets, and I nod. "Cocoa it is." She spreads out again, settling back onto the floor before me.

Cum leaks from her, glistening against the tree lights. I dab at it, swirling everywhere but where she wants my finger. She writhes beneath my touch, but

I don't ease her aches.

Bringing the finger to my mouth, I audibly groan. "You always taste like you're dipped in sugar," I praise, wanting her to know her cum is un-fucking-real.

Grabbing the roll of ribbon, I unwind it. It's green, with little gold plaid sewn in. It's a stark contrast to her, and it only reaffirms that green is the best color on her.

"Legs straight up."

Together, she straightens and raises them. Immediately, I get to work, wrapping it around her. Not too tight to be uncomfortable, but enough to be stable and stiff. I weave back and forth between her legs, starting at her hips. She's going to be my tree, after all.

"What are you doing?"

"It's a surprise," I reassure her, teasingly rubbing her skin with every wrap. She shivers and my body aches with the desperation to sink inside her.

After I've got her weaved from her hips to her ankles, I smile at my handiwork. She peeks up at me, her eyes widening. "I thought I felt fabric of some sort."

Swatting her ass for misbehaving, she lets out a sharp squeal. "That's for peeking, little monster."

"I'm sorry, Santa. Don't put me on the naughty list."

I chuckle at her, knowing that if having a good time fucking people was a mark for the naughty list, anyone who enjoys orgasms would be fucked. Literally and figuratively.

"I want to put you on the naughty list just so I can come back to see you. Then I'll punish you. I'll make sure you're my last stop so I spend every extra moment buried in your cunt.

Her face flushes, her teeth digging into her lip. "Please, I'd like that." I smack her ass again, massaging the sting after.

"I'm sure you would. You'd purposefully misbehave if it meant more orgasms, hmm?" It's a taunt, and she definitely knows how to answer.

She nods, trying to shake her ass. Unfortunately, she's too restrained to do that. "I'd be bad every single day if it meant you were at the end of each punishment."

My chest tightens at her words. It's moments like this that confuse me. She seems enamored, but is it a role for the game we play or something deeper?

I guess I could ask her, but would she be honest? She said she was desperate for love. Would that make her do anything to please me?

I tie the string lights around her, looser than the ribbon, but over it so the heat from the lights doesn't directly touch her skin.

She might like that, though.

Once all the ornaments are in place, I silently tap my shoulder for a job well done. She's on her back, her legs straight up. Wrapped in ribbon, lights, and covered in dangling ornaments, she looks like the perfect Christmas tree.

"Perfection," I let out, not meaning for it to be so loud.

Her eyes finally fly open and she gawks, her expression full of amusement and awe. "I look like my favorite part of Christmas," she breathes.

"Santa wanted his own tree," I explain. "He even wants to fuck his tree."

She smiles, her teeth showing as she enthusiastically nods. "Pretty sure that's against forest code." Her joke has me confused for all of five seconds.

"They don't have any rules against fucking trees, sweetness. Hell, maybe that's why sap exists."

Her mouth drops open and closes. "You win. That's a visual I didn't need."

"Yet, you pictured it."

She attempts to slap my chest but again, but she's stuck from being tied up. "Are you ready, Xóchitl?"

# CHAPTER 21

### BESAME MUCHO — ANDREA BOCELLI

### XO

"Are you ready, Xóchitl?"

I've never felt so wound up and wet. He hasn't pointed it out, but I've been dripping down crassly. It's filthy and slick, and he's just watching as it comes out of me.

Part of me believes it's a kink for him, the other makes me wonder if he wants me to make waves.

It's probably the latter.

"I'm ready, Santa."

He lets out a little growl at my words. I've noticed when I call him Santa, it both turns him on and angers him. The mix is too addictive to ignore.

From behind his back, Arson pulls out an unwrapped candy cane and I wonder what he plans on doing with it.

I don't have to wait long. He weaves it through the front of the ribbon, and it lays directly over my clit.

Oh, goddess.

The sensations already driving through that brief contact have me trembling. It's like the longest edging of my life with this monster. He likes to torment me and I enjoy the way I feel once pure rapture hits me.

"See, that candy cane will tell me how much you're enjoying this. Every time you struggle against your binds, it'll rub that little clit of yours."

I whine as he moves it for me. "This is torture," I cry out as he continues his movements.

"And you fucking love it. Don't you?"

I nod and bite my lip, holding back my whimper. He likes them and if he's torturing me, I'm returning the favor.

As I'm battling with myself over his intent to make me suffer, he's disappeared. "Arson?"

"Shh," he cajoles me, and I feel it. His tongue laves at my entrance, his teeth dragging down my slit too. "Fuck, you're divine."

The praise surprised me at first, but now it's absolutely needed to get me off. Silently demanding him to tell me I'm doing good.

He enters me with his tongue and I jerk, the candy cane hitting me effortlessly. My legs cramp up and from my toes to my head, I tremble.

"Arson!" I cry out, releasing for him. I've not orgasmed that swiftly, ever. It may have only been day three of orgasms, but my last two orgasms were much longer.

"Good, Joyful. You're so pretty when you come."

"Thank you."

His answering chuckle is the only response I get before he's entering me again. The little ridges on the wider point of his tongue have stars shooting behind my eyes. Everything shakes and I'm not sure if it's sensitivity or the fact that I've never used this much of my stomach muscles before. Either way, I'm a wreck already and he hasn't even fucked me.

"Are you scared?" I wonder aloud. "Or do you not want me?"

I've never been doubtful or self-conscious of denial. While I thought I was going to cry yesterday when he would let me touch him, it isn't until this moment that I wonder if he doesn't actually want me. Where this is coming from... who knows.

But this is a job to him, after all.

He sits up, his eyes blazing. Literally. Fire pulsates in his green irises, a volcano readying to erupt. "Scared?" he rasps cruelly. "I'm trying to be gentle, Joyful. Slow, even. Your first time should be—"

"I didn't ask for tender," I respond, not letting him finish his spiel.

"It won't fit if I don't stretch you," he growls, his fingers furiously stroking his massive erection. I still can't get over his candy cane dick. That's wild to me, but I love it.

"It'll fit. But if you're too scared..." I trail off, goading him. He knows it. Irritation flashes in his expression before he's pressing into me. It's sharp and reckless, my entire body tensing at the unfamiliar sensation.

It doesn't hurt too much, and I'm so wet that he slips in easily. "Fuck," he grunts, pushing into me. "Fuck, Xóchitl." He picks up his pace and I squeeze around him as spine-tingling ecstasy fills me. "You're so goddamn good."

His voice comes out animalistic. Inhuman, deep and growly, the veritable monster beneath the surface. "Harder." It's a command, but it's so breathless and frantic. The more he thrusts into me, the more the candy cane works me over.

"Fuck, you're so perfect like this. You take my cock so well, coating it, squeezing..." he trails off, throwing his head back in pleasure. "I won't last long, baby." *Baby.* I literally erupt from that alone, crying out my release as he fucks into me. His cock curves, hitting a star-inducing spot inside me. He doesn't stop until he's roaring and punching into me with so much force my back arches. "Yes, squeeze me just like that." His encouraging words have me squeezing as hard as I can.

"Feel so good... inside me," I brokenly say, wanting to give him what he gives me. "You fill me up so perfectly, Arson. The only one I want is you."

His eyes lock with mine, sweat lining his brow. He grunts a few more times before wetness soaks me, leaking out of me.

"Fuck," he rasps, slowing his pace. His eyes are still flames, burning bright with fervor. He pulls out of me, dipping his fingers inside me. I cry out when he curves his fingers.

"What are you—"

He rises so quickly, I swear his wings flap to assist him. Hovering over me, he presses against my lips. "Taste."

I do.

Licking around his fingers, I moan. I grip them and suck them into my mouth. I lick between them, around them, lapping the flavor off.

Peppermint.

His cum is peppermint.

"It makes sense now," I say after popping out his fingers. He knows what I'm referring to but doesn't comment. "You couldn't stand my coffee because you were thinking about your cum."

His chest heaves as he smirks. Sweat drips down his chest before he's plunging between my thighs again. "It turns me on, seeing my seed spill from you. I want to fill your mouth and then eat it too. He dips and licks at my hole, using his tongue to scoop it out.

"You're going to make me come again," I cry out, feeling another orgasm build. He presses his finger against the candy cane on my clit, moving it in determined circles.

"Come for me, sweetness. Show me how much you want me to fill you up." I move my hips as much as I can and scream as he enters me with several fingers at the same time.

The tingling I've come to appreciate so much hits me again, my entire body shuddering. "Arson," I groan. It's not a scream, but a promise that I cannot stop what we're doing.

# MAEVE BLACK

## CHAPTER 22

### PLEASE COME HOME FOR CHRISTMAS – RYLAND JAMES

### XO

This is it. This is how I die. With my cock inside the woman I'm falling for while my seed spills from her with every thrust.

From head to toe, I've covered her in white. If not for the showers and baths, she'd be as snowy as a candy cane. We've been at it for days. *I think.*

After unwrapping her the other night, I gave her a bath and cuddled her in bed. We're now on her mattress, and I'm inside her. The bed dips with each thrust and my balls ache as I drive into her. I'm holding back until she comes once more. I need to see it.

She writhes beneath me, holding her tits as I stroke her clit slowly. Her body shudders as her orgasm overtakes her and with her squeezing me, I roar out my own release.

"Fuck, sweetness, you're so good."

I pull out, immediately scooping up my cum. Her mouth is already open, waiting for me. I drag my release up her throat and into her waiting mouth. Licking the path from her neck to her lips, I taste myself and her mixed.

There are no words to describe the bliss this woman makes me feel. She moans around my fingers as I press down on her tongue. I could spend the rest of my life inside her, fucking her to completion.

She's perfect.

Perfect for *me*.

She reaches down between us, aiming my cock at her entrance again. Humping upward, she forces me inside and we hiss together as our bodies rock.

"I never thought sex would be this good," she breathlessly admits. Her hand connected to where my cock meets her cunt, dipping inside herself as I enter her. She's intrigued with her own pleasure and the fact that I've brought this out of her is so fucking beautiful that I'm at a loss for words.

I want to tell her that sex isn't this good with just anyone. Only her. She's why it's so addictive and euphoric. I've never come inside someone bare, she's my first, and that's more telling than anything else. All I wanted was for her to experience my cum and taste it. Now that I've experienced it, I don't know how I'll give it up.

I rut into her, pistoning my hips. But instead of ramming her into the mattress again, I pull out and flip her so she's on her knees. Similar to the front of her thighs, the back of them are bruised, too, from the ribbon and her constant tugging.

She still looks like a goddamn present to me.

"What is—"

I slam into her and she nearly stands, her back bowing into my chest. I reach between us, circling her clit. "Goes deeper this way," I rasp, kissing her throat. My incisors extend, salivating, readying to bite her and make her ours. Scraping it against her pulse point, she cries out, shaking around my cock.

I can't contain the feral roar that escapes me as she clenches around me. "I like this, a lot," she breathlessly whispers. "Feels like I'm going to pass out from bliss."

"I'm not done with you, baby. I'm going to be buried inside you until you beg me to stop."

"Never," she argues, and I realize she hasn't chastised me for calling her baby. I can't help it. It feels too natural. Her being mine, even for pretend this feels far too real.

My fingers dig into her hips as I'm pressing her face into the bed with my other hand. Rocking into her, I find my release. Since I can't pierce her skin, tying her to me, I just bite her back and let my cum seep out of her.

Wasting no time, I pull out and raise her ass up higher, licking her cunt, tasting myself inside her. It'll never get old. I could eat her daily and still want more of her.

Instead of only eating her pussy, I trail to her ass, keeping another promise I made to my filthy fucking mind. I lick her asshole and she flinches at the touch.

"Arson, please don't stop."

I won't.

Still, I lick around her rim, then enter her, stretching her pink hole, wanting her to know nothing is off-limits for me.

"Someday, I'm going to fuck you here, sweetness. You'll beg for my cock, and I'll indulge you."

"Please, please, please," she whimpers desperately.

I stretch her, using my cum and hers, teasing the ring of muscles. Pressing inside, she is a ball of whimpers and cries, her pussy leaks all over us both. Dripping.

"You're such a good girl for me," I encourage. "You're leaking all over me. Do you want my cock, baby?"

"Please, Santa. Give me your cock."

"Desperation looks fucking wonderful on you," I growl.

By the second finger, she's pressing backward. It's frantic and so fucking sexy. Right before I'm prepping to add a third finger to stretch her, voices interrupt us.

"Did you leave the TV on?" I ask, knowing she didn't. We've been fucking nonstop for days. Being inhuman, we don't need food to sustain ourselves. Not really. I've lost track of time. It's just been her cunt and my cock on repeat. I'm surprised she's not sore. But like me, she seems ravenous and craven.

"Xóchitl! Where the hell are you?"

"Val, my brother," she whisper-yells, practically eradicating herself from me. "Coming!"

"Not anymore," I grumble, feeling an ache from not sinking inside her ass for the first time. To be continued, I guess.

"He's not supposed to be here," she frantically explains. "Not unless there's a new couple." She hurries to look somewhat presentable, throwing on a robe. And all I do is put a pair of jeans on. I don't care if her brother is here. I'll be dicking down his sister as soon as he leaves.

Hell, the sooner the better.

She walks out first. Even to her brother her flushed skin will give away her exertion. She was literally taking my fingers minutes ago. My cum still leaks from her pussy like a faucet.

"Valentine," she announces, and I wait for only a moment to follow her out.

"I'd say I'm in trouble with you using my full name, but you're the one missing in action, little sis."

"What are you talking about? My next charge isn't until New Year's," she argues, and I come out.

I was going to eavesdrop, but knowing Joyful, she'd let him berate her when it's my fault she's here.

Stepping out without a shirt on probably wasn't the best choice. Xó's brother stands almost as tall as me. Unlike her, he's red. More of a coral than my darker shades, but red nonetheless. He narrows his eyes as anger seeps from him in heaps, even his lip curls in disgust.

"Who the fuck are you?"

Instantaneously, Xó smacks his chest. Her furrowed brow and glare could make a grown man cry. "Don't talk to him that way, Valentine. He's my friend."

"Friend, my ass," Valentine bites out. "He's a fucking Santana."

"Oh, so you must be the Cupid my brother fucked," I mock, folding my arms across my chest. If he were draegyn, his eyes would be blazing. Still, hatred leaks from him rapidly.

"Arson!" Xó chastises, her eyes wide and disappointed. I let out a breath and wait for her move. She's right to give me shit. I'm being senseless. "This is my brother."

"And your sisters," one announces, standing near the door. Her peach skin is subtle and far different from Xó's. Then another one pops out. She's more of a purple color, soft lavender maybe?

"I warned you we'd come. You've been here for weeks."

"Weeks?" she simpers, a grimace transforming her face.

"It's Christmas Eve," he clarifies and my eyes widen. We've been in that bed for much longer than even I realized. It's easy to be lost in each other.

"Shit," I mutter, thinking of how angry Pyro is going to be.

"Shit is right, brother," Pyro exclaims from the kitchen, announcing his presence at the same time. I don't even have time to rub the bridge of my nose before Xó's trembling.

"What the hell were you thinking?"

*Yeah, what the hell were we thinking?*

# CHAPTER 23

### CHRISTMAS WITHOUT YOU – AVA MAX

## XO

My entire body burns as shame licks me like I did Arson consistently. It's brutal in its tantalizing hits, and they all stare at us, waiting for a response.

"He's helping me find love," I timidly answer, my voice a mere squeak. Around my family, I've always felt small, the outcast. Right now, it feels worse, because even Val judges me. I've never seen his jaw this stiff, disappointment in his rigid frame.

"Yeah, *that's* what he's doing," Dion mocks, her lip curled in condemnation.

"Enough," Arson barks out. "Doesn't matter what we were doing. You're all out of line."

Something inside my chest flickers. It's the same tingling that's been here since we met, but at this very moment, it blossoms into something tangible. It fills me with peace. Protectiveness. He's defending me. No one ever defends me.

"Arson's right. Cupids may have their rules about no love and whatever, but they have a deal outside of our purview and it's dumb for us to judge," Pyro parrots, nodding at his brother.

At least Arson has a sibling who loves him. But now that Val glowers at Arson's brother, I wonder if that convoluted comment about them sleeping together is accurate.

"Shut up, Cupid."

"Cupid, how damn original, Jolly boy."

*Jolly boy?*

"Out," I toss at Val and Arson's brother, using my thumb to direct them both out the back door. They let out a disgruntled breath and sidestep us all.

Dion follows suit, hopping with so much delight. Torment has always been her superpower, and right now, she witnessed chaos firsthand that wasn't caused by her for once.

Dulce leans toward my ear, her hands gripping my shoulders. "If I knew he was Santa, I'd be coming too."

"Dulce, you did not just say that!" I balk, gagging at the fact that she's eye-fucking the man I think I might be in love with. I'm going to stab her, I swear to the goddess.

An untempered rage builds inside me and I can't say the words before Arson steps in. "We need a minute."

Grateful for him, I want to kiss him in appreciation. Dulce leaves, sashaying her hips, and my fingers pinch my skin as I fist my hands so hard.

"It's okay, Joyful. I've only got eyes for you," he teases, but I don't need his playfulness. I erupt.

"Why are you such a button pusher?" I hiss, my chest heaving with too many emotions. His eyebrows draw in, fury appearing for the first time directed at me.

"Me? I'm your *friend*," he spits, repeating my words to Val. He's so hulking when he's pissed.

"Arson, I didn't mean—"

"Yeah, and what did you mean?" he presses, his eyes firing up, similar to several days ago when he took my virginity. This is different, though. He's unforgiving, bidden with the type of resentment that makes zero sense.

"We *are* friends?" I say and question all at once. "We have an agreement."

He nods once, sharply, and that nod tells me as much as any argument does. I said the wrong thing, and he's upset.

"I should go," he mutters.

"What about our deal?"

His hackles rise and steam leaves both his nose and mouth. I'm walking on rocks, hovering over the deadliest lava. He lets out a huff before turning away from me.

"I'll find you your love, but I've got to go. It's Christmas Eve, and this is too much for me to deal with right now."

"Arson, please," I beg, an ache forming in my chest. "Let's talk about it."

He turns his head slightly, defeat and a hot temper resting between his eyebrows. "There's nothing to talk about. We're friends, Xóchitl. And our deal is complete."

"How?"

He doesn't offer me a response. He heads to the spare room. I rush for him a moment later, but the window in there is open, and there's nothing left in the room but his hat from that first night.

The only thing that lets me know he wasn't entirely an imposter claiming to be Santa.

What have I done?

Why is expressing my feelings out loud so hard?

I walk outside, my entire body shaking and not from the cold. Something inside me splinters and I wonder if this is what heartbreak is. The other day,

I thought I felt it from the lack of response from Santa's letters, but now, after Arson's departed under bad terms, reality sinks in.

I've always known love isn't an emotion I've experienced. Not until Arson. His leaving didn't anger me. It hurt.

I'm entirely in love with him.

He wasn't just someone I made a deal with. He became the outcome of that deal. I'm so fucking stupid.

"What's wrong, Xóchi?" Dulce questions, and either my face is crestfallen or she's very intuitive.

"He left," I snivel, and she immediately comes to my side. Bringing me into her arms, I simply cry. My sister has never comforted me and now that I'm already raw from Arson, it's too much.

Even Arson's brother and Val stop their argument to see what's wrong.

"He's a hothead," Arson's brother explains. "I'm Pyro." He offers me a nod in acknowledgement. "I'm going to check in on him. Just know he risked everything for whatever thing you agreed to. I don't think he planned on getting so involved."

"What do you mean?" I cry. "This was *his* plan!"

He shakes his head. "I mean, he's definitely in love with you. Whatever you two shared is very real. He's not coping with how you blew it off as a simple game."

I nod, knowing that's where I went wrong. "I love him," I admit, my lip wobbling as the emotion overwhelms me.

"He knows. Arson might be angry and stupid right now, but he knows. Right now, he's got a big night ahead of him. It was nice to meet you. Even if the circumstances were quite shit."

I offer a little laugh and he flies away.

"I hate that guy," Val complains, and I can tell he doesn't truly mean that. His constant preaching of love not existing or whatever was him speaking from experience.

One day, they'll both realize it.

"Let's get you washed up, then you can tell us all the dirty details."

"Absolutely not," Val admonishes while Dion shakes her head with horror.

"Okay, maybe *we'll* discuss all the dirty deets," she conspiratorially whispers in my ear. "Then you can tell us how big of a ho, ho, ho you were for Santa. There's no way you're not on the naughty list."

I groan at Dulce's amusement, wishing they had stayed away. I easily could've lived in Arson's arms and legs for so much longer.

Maybe even forever.

# CHAPTER 24

## LAST CHRISTMAS — WHAM!

# ARSON

"You're dumb," Pyro says hours later once we're home. I'm dressed in my normal clothes, and he shakes his head. "Maybe you didn't find your Christmas spirit."

I think of Xó, of her pinkness and pure love for this time of year, how she celebrated all the little things, and, through her eyes, it felt like I was a kid again.

It's there.

The soul of Christmas, and it's all because she reminded me of what was missing. Love. Her love for the holidays drove me to want to be better.

"Give me the list."

"I already checked it," Pyro grumbles, his eyes rolling at my sudden mood shift.

"Yeah, but you never check twice, you fuck. Also, Xó made fun of me for not checking it once and especially not twice. I'll never live it down."

"You won't live long if you don't apologize for rushing out of there. I haven't seen you that worked up, ever."

"I love her, man."

He nods. "Yeah, no shit, Sherlock. It's obvious you're both mad about each other."

I shake my head in denial. "I'm just a stepping stone for her finding her happy ending."

Pyro walks directly to me and smacks the back of my head. "Yeah, definitely stupid. *You* are her happy ending. She literally started crying the moment you left. You've hurt her and if you don't fix this, you'll regret it for the rest of your life. And that's a long-ass time, Arson."

"Shit."

He shakes his head and throws the tablet at me. *Yeah, they do the lists on tablets now.*

I scroll freely, and when my hand hovers Xó's name, warmth fills me up.

*Nice.*

Guess she's been a good girl, after all.

I scan the list for everyone, making sure there's nothing out of place. Then I do it again, speeding through this time.

There are so many people on these lists that have switched from naughty to nice, but a part of me knows that I've been dwelling on that for far too long.

Christmas is so much more than my fears.

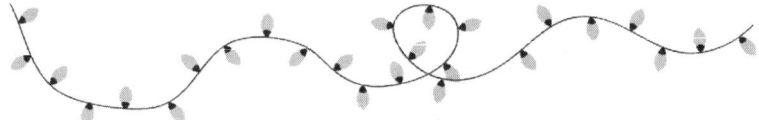

The shop isn't different, but somehow, I'm seeing it in a different light. Like every year, it's covered in rich colors. Emeralds, golds, and especially the classic ruby red. Ornaments are hung, wreaths decorate every door, and there's so much more tinsel than necessary.

The Ranish people—or elves, as humans call them—work tirelessly. Their smiles are full of cheer. It's something I haven't noticed in years.

Their cheeks are rosy, full of life, and when they see me walking through the entryway, they pause.

"Santa!" Trouble and Mayhem, the twins, shout. Then everyone's coming toward me with excitement. "You're here!"

They all tell me about how the build of everything has been seamless and everyone's toys are prepared. There have been changes and Pyro has been walking them through the expectations. I'll never be able to thank him enough for picking up my slack for me.

"I appreciate you all," I announce. Their expressions shift from excitement to sentimental. "This last week, I found someone I can finally call my Mrs. Claus."

Cheers break out and they jump. Slowly, I scan the room, seeing the same joy that Xó constantly exudes.

"What's her name?"

"Xóchitl," I immediately answer, pride lacing my tone. "She's actually Cupid."

"Cupid's real?!" The shouts ringing out have me chuckling.

"She is and while I know tradition tells me to marry and step down, I think for at least one winter, if she'll have me, we'll do this together."

Their eyes glisten. A mixture of pride and awe fills them. She's the true spirit of Christmas. With her, I might be able to make a difference. Then when she's ready to have babies, Pyro can take his place as Santa.

Sometimes, I wonder if that's even what he wants or if we should offer it to our younger brother, Blaze. He's never around. Hell, he runs around the world sticking his dick in every person he can.

We haven't seen him in years, especially since his duties don't even begin until far after Pyro settles down.

Then there's the youngest, Cinder. We won't even start on him. He's not even remotely ready.

"When can we meet her?" Lars, one of the workers, asks, his face filled with hope. They truly want this for me and themselves.

"As soon as I convince her that she's mine."

"Sounds like you've got your work cut out for you," Pyro announces from above the balcony. Pride settles in his eyes. They're nearly glowing, something he never offers. Especially not to me.

For years, I've been bitter. The last three hundred or so, I've been on this throne—so to speak.

"She really wants to meet the drakes," I tell them, almost like she's a story. They peer at each other with amusement. "Think she'll want to nest an egg?"

Something I never told her is that when drakes are ready to create, they lay eggs. These eggs are given to every draegyn to take care of and make sure they are born.

Then after we do that, they go with the other drakes, no strings attached. It's almost a special part of this entire thing. A hidden secret she'll probably lose her shit over.

They all nod enthusiastically. "When are you having a baby?" Harpy yells, her vibrant purple eyes catching mine in the crowd.

Chuckling, I shake my head. "Whenever she's ready, we'll have one."

"Think they'll be pink or ugly red like you, brother?" Pyro taunts, his amusement apparent. I flip him the bird and stick out my tongue.

"Don't be jealous, brother. Maybe Val will let you inside again."

He gets the innuendo immediately, hatred firing his eyes up. Yeah, he's a goner for my woman's Cupid brother.

"Maybe you should deal with that anger, can't be burning down the shop with your celibacy." Now, it's his turn to return his middle finger.

He grumpily walks off, and after I say goodbye to the Ranish fae, I follow suit.

By the time I've made it back to my room, after spending a week away, I notice a red envelope on my bed. It has a little sticky note attached to it.

And I read.

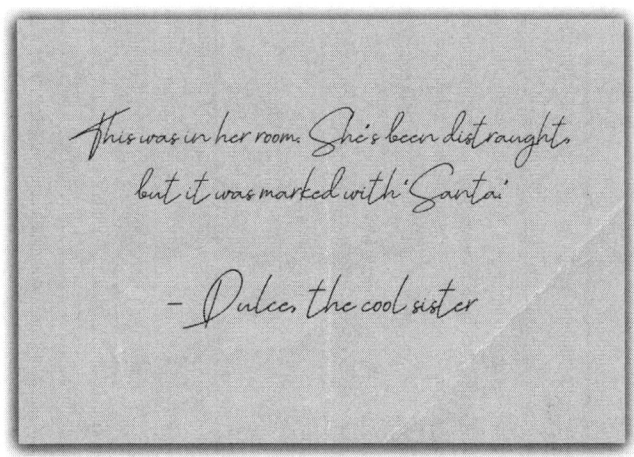

*This was in her room. She's been distraught, but it was marked with 'Santa.'*

*— Dulce, the cool sister*

I laugh at the note and rip the seal. Inside is easily the saddest letter I've read. It's the last letter she wrote before I showed up. One lacking all hope she had the entire time we were together. I've only proven that like her thoughts, she wasn't good enough.

She's more than deserving of love, and as I told her before, I'd find her that love, no matter what.

Pangs of disappointment hit me as I acknowledge it's the Eve of Christmas. If I don't deliver the world their presents and wishes, it'll destroy them.

But I know deep within me, if I don't go after her, I'll lose her forever.

With a plan formulating in my mind, I pack another to-go bag and decide exactly what I'll be doing tonight.

# CHAPTER 25

I'LL BE HOME – MEGHAN TRAINOR

## XO

It's been hours and I've begged my siblings to leave me. They stayed for a while, making sure I was stable. After yelling at them, they agreed to take my two new charges before leaving.

The cottage is lonely. It's filled with the decorations we put up, the tree we picked together, and inside my fridge still sits the dough from days ago.

Knowing it's still okay to use, I grab my apron and put it on. Tying the green straps, I remember the last time I'd done it.

It was the night I lost my virginity. Every part of me knows the moment I met Arson, there was a spark. It was love.

Whether that had to do with me being Cupid or him being Santa, I'm unsure. All I do know is that thinking of spending Christmas and every other day without him hurts worse than anything I've ever experienced.

A knock sounds at my door, interrupting my turmoil. I make my way toward the front, emotions clogging my throat.

I've never been much of a drinker, but right now, a nice glass of spiked eggnog sounds delightful.

"Coming!" I yell at whoever's on the other end of the door. Clamoring for the knob, I turn it. No one stands there, but on the ground is a package.

It's pink, wrapped, and somehow, I know it's for me.

*It's pink, obviously.*

Crouching, I look for a note and don't see one. Pink and pretty, I wonder who wrapped it and if it was Arson.

Hope blooms in my chest at the thought, and I carry it inside to unwrap. As I tug at the corner, excitement has me fidgeting.

Impatience goads me to rip it open and not care about keeping the paper pretty. And I listen. I don't even go in any direction, I simply pull.

Inside sits a pink box, and on top of it is a pink envelope. It's not the same as the ones I've been sending Santa, but it's still pretty.

Picking it up first, I smile. It's labeled with 'Cupid.' Untucking the unsealed flap, I pull out the card.

It's not a letter, it's a Christmas card. On the front is a bunch of glittery reindeer and the cursive words, *'Twas the night before Christmas.*

Flipping it open, a few sentences appear as if they're magic. Spelling the words out as my eyes read them.

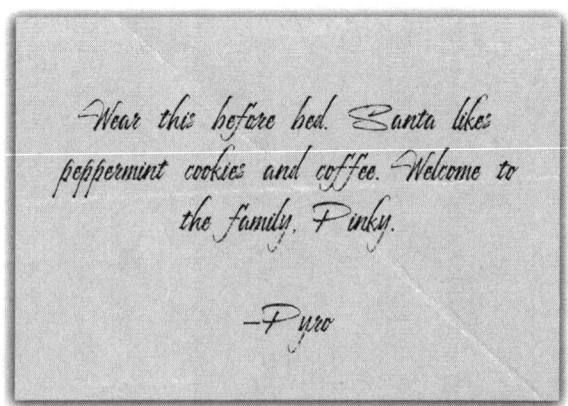

Placing the card down, I open the box. Inside is a sinfully red baby doll. If

Arson realizes his brother sent me this, it'll be his funeral. Aside from that, my elated heart beats with the thought that Arson will be coming here tonight.

He didn't simply abandon me.

Deep down, I knew he wanted me. It's an inescapable feeling, love. To think I was ever safe from its thrall is naïve at best.

I grab the box and put it in my bedroom, knowing that after I make the gingerbread cookies, I'll be making a special recipe for my Monster Claus.

And maybe, just maybe, Santa will be *coming* for Christmas.

Later, after I've kneaded the dough and cooked it to perfection, I start on the peppermint cookies. I crush a bunch of candy canes in a bag, appreciating the little slivers perfectly shaped for the treats.

I make a sugar cookie dough, one that has a little bit of nutmeg and white cocoa added in. After the peppermint flakes are in it, I put it in the fridge to sit.

It feels like forever once all the cookies are done. But during that time, I whip up the thick icing for the gingerbread, knowing that I'll be forcing Arson to experience this. Even if only once.

Night comes too slowly, but I make sure to dress in the nightie. Unfortunately, I fall asleep before setting the cookies out for him.

"Xóchitl, baby," a voice rouses me from my sleep. I grumble at being woken mid-dream, but the winter wonderland in my sleep begged me to go back. "You've always loved your sleep." Amusement laces the tone of the voice and I pout.

"Five minutes, having the best dream of my draegyn," I sleepily groan. A warm hum has me blinking my eyes slowly open.

Above me, Arson stands. He's donning a Santa suit. Shock fully wakes me up. I sit up, seeing his pants tented and his eyes ablaze.

He has on brown trousers, a huge red blazer with white filigree trimming it.

His horns poke through the hat, and his wings somehow have little twinkling lights on them.

I rub at my eyes, swearing that I'm imagining him. There's no way he's dressed to the nines in a Christmas getup.

"It's me, Joyful," he responds to my inner monologue.

"You look like Santa," I proudly respond, wiping at the emotion slipping free. He falls to his knees, his hands clasping my thighs.

"Merry Christmas," he emotionally rasps. "I brought your gift." I shake my head immediately. If he thinks he can give me some random-ass man, he's wrong. I know what I want.

"Arson—" I try to argue and he silences me with his hand.

"Let me explain," he begs, his eyebrows dipping inward. With an accepting nod, I wait for what he has to say. "I love you, Xóchitl. I think the moment I read your letters, my love for you started to form." He leans forward, placing his forehead against mine. "I was desperate to find what had been missing for years. When you fell from that ladder, I knew you were somehow the answer to my prayers."

He places a kiss on top of my head, then we're eye to eye. His eyes flame and I don't think I'll ever get use to it.

"One reason I immediately adored you was the sass. You always fought back and put me in my place. Then you wanted lessons in love, and each time, I gave you a part of myself."

"I love you too," I whisper out as he kisses my jaw. Adoration traces his face as his smile widens.

"I want you, forever. Here, the North Pole, any place you'll have me."

Warmth spreads through me like an overspilling volcano, it's hot and heady, a promise. I grab his face, bringing it to mine. He rumbles as I force my tongue between his lips.

It's so deep and desperate. More strength than I currently have, he separates us. "What's this?" he asks as he tugs on my matching outfit to his. It's literally the naughty version of his outfit, but my baby doll is red with fluffy white edging.

"A gift," I tease. "Pyro dropped it off..." I clench my teeth, exposing them with an awkward smile. He growls, his claws extending from his fingers. With precise movements, he entirely slices it off me.

"Much better," he bites out, his voice sounding more monster than man. I'm sitting on the couch that started it all, naked and ready.

"So you want me?" I push, wanting him to reassure me some more. Him leaving hurt me more than I care to admit.

He nods sharply, his claws retracting. "The first time we kissed, I already knew I'd never be able to give you up. I just didn't think it was real."

"It's real," I promise, tracing his lips with my thumb. He nips at me and leans in. "Make me yours, for real this time."

"You don't have to tell me twice."

## CHAPTER 26

### WHERE ARE YOU CHRISTMAS – FAITH HILL

## ARSON

"Can I?" she shyly asks, reaching for my wing. Her pink fingertips pause in midair, waiting for my response. I give her a reassuring nod.

They stretch as far as she can, but my wings are too far out of her reach with her laying on the sofa. I move them inward, inching toward her waiting hand.

Her eyes gloss over as emotion fills her. When we meet in that way, her skin soft and my wing weathered, I let out the lowest and pleased hum known to the realm.

It's from within me, my draegyn clawing its way out, desperate for the connection. She brushes me, it's so gentle, sensual even.

"They're so beautiful," she offers, teasing the sensitive flesh with slow movements. I can't hold back the groan and how my cock inflates at her touch.

"Please stop," I urgently rasp, my body shuddering with pleasure: It's not only the most intimate thing we've done, it's also hot as fuck.

Playfulness gleams in her pink orbs, her intentions clear. She sits up, darting her tongue out. Before I can stop her, she's licking a long stripe across me and I'm buckling to my knees. *Fuck.*

"Xóchitl," I darkly rumble, quaking from the little movement. She doesn't heed my warning, instead, she runs her palms across the lights I've attached, removing them while my body shakes from head to toe.

She doesn't stop there. Her hands grip me and it's the same feeling my cock gets when she licks at it. "Fuck, fuck, fuck."

It comes out rushed and hotly, I'm at the edge of my control, and I think she knows that. Her smile tells me she's enjoying having control.

After the lights are gone, she goes for my red shirt. Her hands trace each ridge of my muscles, like she's tracing it to memory. I raise my arms, assisting her as she stands. Pulling at the material, she makes sure to be agonizingly slow.

"Good boy," she praises, and I nip at her hip, since it's bare and within reach. A moan leaves her and I know she's winding herself up too.

She taps my hat for good measure and kisses my forehead. "That can stay, Santa." I nip at her throat too, and the most sultry sound leaves her. "You going to bite me, Monster Claus?"

"Only if you want to be bound forever. Draegyns mate for life, Joyful."

Hope blossoms in her gaze. "Then you'll bite me... tonight."

My control snaps with her words. There's no restraint left after that. I'm claiming her. She squeaks as I stand, taking her with me.

No couch tonight. Tonight, we're messing up her sheets. I practically run to the bed and lay back, taking her with me.

"Sit on Santa's lap, baby," I encourage. This time, there's no hesitation. She moves my cock to her entrance and slides down. Her hands don't rest on my chest, though. No, they flatten over my spread wings.

Using them as her leverage, she slides up and down me. Her ass hitting me when she plops down. It's so fucking wet, the slapping sounds of our bodies as she uses me.

"I want this every day," she demands with punctuated hops. My cock throbs with her wrapped around it, and she could ask for anything as long as she doesn't stop her movements. "Say it." Her words are pinched but she hovers over the top of my cock, not sliding down. My tip throbs as she barely works it over.

"Every day," I promise. "Whatever you want."

"I want to fuck you in your sleigh," she adds, tapping her chin. She's sliding down so fucking slow that I'm near combustion from the tension alone.

"Done," I rasp, begging that she slides back up. She starts to, then stops.

"I want to meet the drakes," she barters, giving me a slow and clenched draw up my shaft. Mischief is the only expression she offers as my half-lidded pleasured gaze meets hers.

"They're here," I grunt out. "The sooner you come for me, the sooner you'll meet them."

She pauses at the top of me again, teasing my cockhead with her hovering cunt. She's being a little minx, controlling my pleasure like I've done to her several times.

Heat blooms in my chest as she reaches for my balls. She massages, squeezing, then as she fists them, she slides down me ever so slowly.

"Fuck, sweetness."

"That's what I'm doing, Santa. Fucking you."

"Filthy mouth," I grumble, loving that she's now willing to say the words.

"Must be all the peppermint cum," she taunts, hopping on me quickly. The bouncing of her tits above me and the clenching of her pussy around me has me erupting. I roar, letting her fuck me. She moans with me, shaking as she takes her own pleasure.

Before she can run off to meet the drakes, I grab her. With a little fumbling, I bring her pussy to my mouth.

She sits on my face backward as I lick her cunt. Above me, she writhes and whimpers. "Arson," she moans. "I want to meet them." I can hear the pout in her voice, but I won't have it. It's Christmas and I'm taking my gift by the mouthful.

I don't stop lapping at her leaking hole, and I'm making sure to flick her clit just enough to make her tremble.

"You're going to be a good girl and let me eat. It's been nearly a day, Joyful. I need my fill, and you need to give it to me."

She whines above me, but grinds down on my waiting mouth. I don't even guide her but she reaches for my cock, surprising me.

Her tongue laves the stem, her teeth biting along her way to my head. I curve it, letting her have her favorite candy cane.

She moans, vibrating my cock as she sucks me down the best she can. Her drool leaks down my length, dripping to my lower stomach.

Sloppy noises sound out as she continues her desperate movements, and I double down, sticking my middle and index fingers inside her while eating her out like it's my last supper.

We both hum as our orgasms build. I bite at her ass, knowing that's next on my do-to list. She rocks against my face, and I know she's so close.

I lay my tongue flat, the ridges exposed, and I let her hump my face to completion. She doesn't pop off my cock to beg me, but I straighten it and she chokes it down. The mixture of suction and my fingers inside her have me roaring out my release.

Her hips bounce her cunt on my tongue in a tap, tap, tap motion and she sucks down my cum with a groan. And as soon as I wrap my lips around her clit, pushing on her g-spot, she cries around my length, garbling and choking out her release.

Her entire body shudders above me. From head to toe she trembles, and then it comes out, coating my chest. I reach up to place my lips open like a waiting mouth.

Her orgasm squirts into my mouth like a fucking fountain, spraying my tongue while I swallow it down.

It keeps going as her body quakes. "That's right, Joyful. Give it all to me." I continue to lave at her clit, making sure every drop is licked up.

She cries, her little whimpers so strong and needy. "Arson, what the fuck was that?" Helping her rotate on me, her eyes are watery with tears.

"That, my love, was squirting."

"That felt so weird," she whispers, shame flaming her cheeks.

I kiss her cum-covered mouth, using my thumb to swirl the dripping drool over her lips. "It was perfect. A perfect gift for Santa."

The praise has her melting in my arms, and we stay like that, holding each other. This was the best Christmas I've ever had, and I even got the girl out of it.

# CHAPTER 27

### FELIZ NAVIDAD — JOSE FELICIANO

## ARSON

I don't even let her sleep. On bated breath, I wait for her to recover before flipping her onto her back.

"One more," I urge. Kissing her throat, down her stomach, and thighs. I come back to her breasts, realizing I've neglected them tonight. Flicking my tongue across her nipple, I swirl. She bows into me, her eyes closing as pleasure takes her.

"One more, Joyful. Then you can meet the drakes." She nods slowly.

"Only one?"

I smirk, thinking of how she usually goes twice in quick succession. "However many you do before I come."

"Arson," she grumbles, but her eyes are heated. She's insatiable, just like me.

"Fine, but you have to promise to bite."

"I fucking swear it, sweetness."

She smiles that dopey smile reserved just for me and I sink inside her.

Bowing upward, she groans. Like me, she probably aches from our marathon of fucking this last week.

After several thrusts, she's perspiring freely. Her baby hairs framing her face are soaked, sticking to her skin. I pull out, sinking down to her.

"I was going to bend you over for this part," I explain, dipping my tongue in her wet hole. It's filled with peppermint and sugar, my favorite. "But, I want to fuck your ass while looking at you fall apart."

She whimpers. "I don't think I can take another one." It's almost a plea, soft and tortured, but I know she can.

"You're going to come, baby. You're going to take my cock too." She nods, biting her lip, and I use my fingers to gather our cum.

She's soaked, still leaking like a fountain. I drag it to her little pink hole, stretching it with each pass of cum. It molds to my fingers, and I scissor them to soften the muscles.

"More," she begs, leaning on her elbows to watch me stretch her. She's a demanding little thing.

"As you wish, my love," I concede, pressing another finger inside. We're up to three fingers, lots of cum, and as I pull back a little, I release a lot of drool over her hole. Perfection. A sloppy hole for me to fill.

"Arson, please," she whines, shuddering again. She's so on edge, I bet her stomach is all cramped and tight. That's what edging does, frazzles the entire system.

Once she's all loose, I line my cock up with her entrance. I ease in, not wanting to hurt her on a quick thrust.

She reaches for my ass, pulling me closer. When I'm fully seated, she lays back. "Please fuck me."

"You're going to get on the naughty list with that mouth," I tease, drawing out and punching forward. My hips meet her thighs and she cries out louder than I've ever heard before.

"Punish me then. Santa punishes bad girls, yes?" she taunts me right back, holding her boobs, teasing her own nipples.

I can't handle the sight.

Spine-tingling heat fills me as I lean forward, taking one into my mouth. I nip and bite at it, leaving little hickeys on her cleavage. Fuck, she's perfect with shades of me painting her.

"You're mine, Xóchitl. My love, my future wife, and my mate," I confess, leaning into her throat. "Forever."

My incisors lengthen as I rut my hips and hover over her pulse point. The point of this bite isn't for blood exchange like most fae. No. It's about the permanent mark she'll carry of mine.

Pulsations overtake my cock as I break the skin of her throat. She cries out, but not in pain, in pleasure. As her blood fills my mouth, my balls throb and I start my fury of thrusts. Her hands come to my face and my wings pin them beneath me. I have to hold my incisors inside her for a moment for the tether to take place.

I fuck her and use my thumb to trace her clit gently, like I'm coaxing a secret out of her. Heat burns through my throat and the tingling of our bond hums through me and into her bite as we both chase our releases with our sloppy hip thrusts and movements.

She screams as our bond locks into place, snapping like an overstretched rubber back. My cock twitches several times before I'm seated inside her.

Cum leaks from me and doesn't stop, it's like a shower of peppermint. Her cries continue as she trembles beneath me. Finally letting her move, she pushes against my chest to flip us and I help her climb on top of me.

She hops up and down my length, still chasing her orgasm. Leaning down as she takes me deeper, she bites me back. Her teeth aren't sharp like mine, but she keeps going until it breaks the skin right above my heart.

"Fuck," I groan. The pain isn't much, it's the love rushing through our bond that has me wrecked.

"I-I'm so sorry," she apologizes, her lips covered in blood. Probably a match to my own. "There was this demand in my chest, it was almost fiery, forcing me to bite."

I've never heard of a draegyn bond bringing forward another's mate through it, but with how she described it, I almost wonder if that's the case.

"I love you," I repeat my earlier words. "Will you be my wife, too?"

Her eyes shine with tears as she frantically nods. "Yes."

IF YOU DON'T LIKE BABIES,
ONLY READ EPILOGUE ONE.

# EPILOGUE ONE

## LITTLE SAINT NICK – THE BEACH BOYS

## XO

Snow covers the hilltops. White reflects off every surface, so bright and perfect for Christmas. After Arson and I completed the bond, there was nothing else I wanted than to cuddle. Something shifted in that moment. It felt like a snap of some sort in my chest. The emotions filling me reflected my own.

He loves me.

It's love.

The one thing I sought after for so long is now mine.

"Good morning, Monster Claus," I announce. He's naked from head to toe, his chest bruised from my biting mouth. I'm standing in front of my window, watching as the valley piles up with more snow.

His arms wrap around my middle, his mouth kissing my throat. I hum, feeling my body heat from the comfort. "Good morning, mate."

*Mate.*

Shivering, I rotate into him, taking his mouth with mine. He groans, his tongue teasing mine. "Are they cold out there?" I interrupt his growing erection at my back. With his own complaint, he nips my cheek.

"No, they don't get cold. But they're fine."

"How do you know, you left them all alone!" I'm not angry but feel the need to be chastising because I think of them as any animal out in the cold.

"Xóchitl, baby, I promise they're fine. I'm sure they're excited to meet you. The Ranish were talking about how you're on the nice list—"

"I'm on the nice list?!" I shout with utter joy. I'm on the *nice* list!

"Yes, you definitely are. After all, you were the *best* girl for Santa."

His body emanates heat, warming my back, and I know where this will lead if I don't push to go meet the drakes.

"I'll be a good girl for Santa. Later," I challenge, pulling away. A spark of determination lights behind his green eyes, and I know he'll hold me to that.

"Fine, you can meet the drakes and then I'll fuck you in my sleigh."

I shake my head immediately. "We have to meet your elves." He lets out a complaining grumble, his pouting adorable.

"I think they'll love you," he says, a spark of pride there. He's truly the loveliest monster.

"You think?"

His returning nod is sharp and absolute. "I love you, Xóchitl. There's no doubt they'll love you too."

Our bond warms, a comfort, and then he's pulling me against his chest. The pull to him through our mind is so new, it's something I want to have forever. It's not only reassurance, it's love. It's a constant reminder that no matter what they say about Cupids, we're meant to find love.

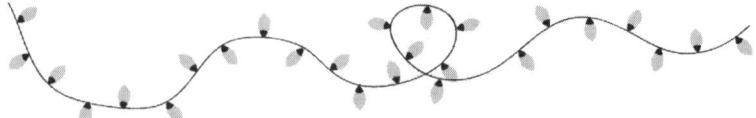

After showering—which Arson argued against because he wanted me to have his scent everywhere—we head outside. The snow crunches beneath my boots and before long, Arson's lifting me wedding style and flying.

My heart hammers as we rise above my house. "This is insane!"

His gaze meets mine, and there's this fierce protectiveness there reflecting back at me. It reminds me so much of when he defended me in front of my siblings. I can't describe the way my chest swells. It's indescribable.

He lands on top of my roof, and to my happiness, there are eight reindeer. Within moments, their bodies change in front of me.

No longer stands reindeer, instead are what anyone would describe as dragons. They're small, all different colors, but the one that's a pure black with pink eyes... that one draws me in.

"That's Amaris," Arson whispers against my neck. His hands cup my hips as he guides me nearer. Amaris blinks slowly at me, as if gauging my intentions. Unwilling to come off as anything but entirely enamored, I drop to my knees, bowing my head.

Heat brushes over my hair, a loud puff of it tickling the strands framing my face. I don't look up, not yet. Then what I can only describe as a snout bumps my cheek. Opening my eyes, I'm met face to face with absolute beauty.

Her scales are sharp, like a jaded heart with edges, and her deep breathing tells me I'm not being treated like a threat.

Tentatively, I reach out for her. She flinches initially, her concern apparent. Eventually, her eyes close as I'm reaching out to her, and then she blindly presses against my palm.

Tears form in my eyes as a feeling somewhat similar to what I have with Arson infiltrates my chest. It's different in the respect that drakes can't communicate with words. Like the legends of real wyverns, they're mostly animal. Sure, they can glamour like any fae, but their communication is mind based.

Emotions.

Feelings.

Not words.

"She's chosen you," Arson explains to me. His hand presses into my back, comforting me.

"Chosen?" It's one word, but it feels so heavy. Placing my hand on her head, I gently pet her. She presses into my touch, letting out a chirping sound.

"You're hers now. No matter what happens in life, she'll protect you. And when she's ready to bear children, you'll nest her egg."

All this information settles inside me, an overwhelming sense of peace consumes me. I've always had this tug toward Draegyn. It's a place that's no more in Darchon—yet it's always enticed me.

"They always say the Fates have no love for beings, it's simply given guidance by its inner self. But here, now, how this turned out, I think the Fates have a soft spot." Standing, I give Amaris one last head pat and turn to my monster. "I think the Fates couldn't keep us apart."

"They are kind," Arson offers. "They chose you for me; they knew you were my perfect match."

Emotion drips from my eyes, and before he takes my mouth, he swipes each tear from my cheeks. "Let's go home, Joyful. The North Pole could use your Christmas cheer."

# MAEVE BLACK

# EPILOGUE, TOO

### CHRISTMAS CANON — TRANS-SIBERIAN ORCHESTRA

## ARSON

**W**e fly home, the wind chilling her to the bone. She snuggles into me, and I warm her with my embers. It's easy to do, bring her heat.

"He's here!" Benjamin, one of the Ranish scouts broadcasts. The bells go off, announcing my arrival, and Xó sits next to me in awe. Her eyes are full of this childlike bliss. She's technically seeing this reality for the first time.

Santa is real, and he's about to be her husband.

"Is this her?" Riah shouts with wonder, her eyes bright and purple. She's one of our youngest elves. Roaming up and down Xó, the glee in her expression seems to only increase.

"This is her," I confirm. "Get the others."

She hops up and down before rushing to the other tower. The chime of the bells doing their little confirmation melody has my chest squeezing with hope.

The entire village starts hitting their bells, communicating their message. *Santa is here!*

After I told them about Xó and how I wanted her as my wife, they knew she was the one for me. I've never once shared about my dating life—or lack thereof.

Suddenly, as the tune of Christmas rings out, elves line up. They run up the arch to the dome we landed in. We're basically inside a massive snow globe.

Hundreds upon hundreds of elves have shown up. Their faces range from awestruck to surprised. Some appear to be in love, and others have the absolute biggest expressions of hope.

When Pyro's flying form comes from the distance, I know it's time.

Turning to my Joyful, I kneel at her feet. Her eyes immediately go to my sunken form. "Arson?" Her voice is filled to the brim with emotion. She's done this a million times for others. There's no doubt she definitely knows I'm here forever.

"Xóchitl Amor, we've not known each other for long, but I love you. Sure, it's quick, but I'm mad about you. I want you to be mine in every way possible. And today, I want you to become my wife."

"Arson," she whimpers, tears sliding down her flushed cheeks. Her emotions play like an orchestra on her face. Through our bond, she's filled with hope and love. "Yes."

I place the ring I had them create before I left onto her ring finger. "I'll spend forever earning you, baby." Her eyes drip while she frantically nods.

Standing, I lift her by the backs of her thighs, kissing her until we're breathless. When our eyes meet again, there's nothing but love reflected at me.

"I love you," I repeat, kissing her forehead, then again her lips. Cheers erupt around us. The elves clapping and jumping.

"I love you too, Arson. I can't believe this is real life."

"I told you I'd find you love," I tease, nuzzling her throat where I bit her last night. It smells of me, her scent melting into it too. "Just didn't know it'd be me."

"I'm glad," she whispers. "You taught me how to please you, after all. Not anyone else."

I growl into her pulse point. "Need you. Now."

"Looks like we're needed elsewhere," Pyro announces, noticing the change in the air. He unfastens the drakes and they fly off. Then all the elves laugh and cheer as they disperse back to their departments.

My body sweats as heat overpowers me. It's something I've only heard about in tales. The shift in one after they've mated.

"They're gone," she whispers. When I pull back, her eyes turn into saucers. "What's happening?" My body melts inside, the heat building and building.

"How much do you want little babies, sweetness?"

Her eyes soften, like melted chocolate over candy cane dipped pretzels. She's biting her lip as my cock hardens worse than ever before.

"More than anything," she admits. "Now tell me why your eyes are only fire, there's literally no green left."

"It's a rut of sorts. We call it melting."

"That sounds... painful?"

"It can be, if I don't get inside you."

She giggles and raises an eyebrow. "What does it mean?"

"When we mate, on a rare occasion, we going into a melt. During that time, we're in a constant state of sex. We have to fill our mates. Over and over," I rasp, feeling pleasure rush over my balls. "We even swell inside. It's the need to breed."

She shivers, her body trembling. "I can feel your desire in our bond."

"I need you, Xó. Right now. If you don't want to bear our child so soon, I'll figure out how to undo this."

Xó shakes her head immediately. "I want this. You. A baby. Fuck me," she brokenly answers, heat zapping back at me through our bond. I don't waste another second, I lift her, flying through the sky. As much as the sleigh would have been fun, it's not big enough for the mess of our soon-to-be shuddering limbs.

We get to my room in the village within moments and I'm rushing inside. She doesn't complain as my claws shred our clothes.

"Arson," she whimpers as I squeeze her breasts. "Please."

I lift her and she wraps her legs around me. Then I'm slamming home. I'm standing, thrusting inside her, and my cock aches to release. She moans when I grip her hips for leverage.

I carry us to the bed, sinking in her as soon as we're fully on it. She squeezes me, her moans filling my entire system with bliss.

Usually, I'd take my time with her, but the melt builds and I can't stop the quick and harsh pace of my cock.

Soon after, I explode with a roar, filling her. She moans and I use my fingers to get her off. We rock together as my seed spills inside her and leaks. No waste.

I pull out, shoving every bit back inside her. The need to lick her, eat our cum, it overwhelms me. Reaching for her clit, I wrap my lips around it and she cries out with her orgasm.

I don't stop, I use my finger to hold my cum inside her and lick her fiercely. The need to stay here forever is planted in my brain, but I know it's the madness of the rut.

After she's literally crying from being oversensitive, I rise and sink inside her again.

"You take my cock so good," I praise, kissing her sweat-covered forehead. "Such a good girl, making me come so fast."

She whimpers. "It's so hot, I need you to fill me. Please. I can't describe it, but I need more."

I know what she needs. Like omegas in heat, she'll crave my swollen cock. It's similar to a knot, holding my cum inside her as I rut.

"Please, Arson. Please," she cries out, tears filling her eyes.

I pull back and slam home. "You want my seed?" She frantically nods, sweat sliding down her temple. "I'll give you my cum, baby. Then I'll swell inside you."

"Yes, that. I need that. Please," she whimpers and we rock together, chasing this high. Her whimpers meet me thrust for thrust.

"You're doing so good, baby. You're so fucking wet. Can you come for me again?"

"No, no, no," she mumbles, squeezing me. "Too much."

I kiss her tear-stained cheeks. "One more. Come for me one more time and I'll come. I'll fill you up, okay?"

"I can't," she whimpers. "Feels too good." I reach between us, placing featherlight circles over her clit. She convulses as she screams in pleasure. And soon, when my incisors elongate, sinking into her throat, she screams her release.

The way she clenches me has me seeing stars, and I explode. The swelling I've heard about forms at the base of my cock, locking me inside her.

Pleasure zips through me as I spill inside her, it's overwhelming and fast. It stays and sends shock waves through my balls.

"What's that?" Xó practically moans it. "Feels like heaven."

"My knot, kind of. They don't have a name for it."

"Love that, want more of that." She groans as it pulses. She rocks against me. "Is this feeling going to stop?"

"What feeling, sweetness?"

"Like I need your cock in every hole, filling me, giving me orgasms?"

I shake my head. "Not entirely, though the melt is making it ten times more pronounced. It'll only get worse. I'm sure for the next week or so, we'll be in here fucking nonstop."

"Mmm," she moans. "I enjoy fucking."

"Dirty girl with a dirty fucking mouth."

"Your fault," she whispers, squeezing my length. "You're the teacher."

"Got me there," I tease, kissing her throat. She bleeds from where I bit her and a little bit of guilt hits me.

"Will our babies look like you?" she questions with wide eyes. "They'll be cute with horns?"

I nod. "Or they'll be adorable, like you, with pink skin and curls."

"Both?"

"We can keep going until we've got both," I promise. "Not like practice is so hard."

She nods and begins to fall asleep. It'll take some time for me to deflate, but at some point, I fall asleep too.

## EPILOGUE: THIRD TIME'S THE CHARM

### CHRISTMAS CANON — TRANS-SIBERIAN ORCHESTRA

### XO

"**D**addy!" Román yells, his dark-as-his-dad's red head bouncing from his little run. I sit with Ash, feeding her. Arson's making the perfect pieces for our gingerbread houses. Since having our Román, he's been really into the Christmas season.

Sure, I brought that initial spark back, but seeing him with our son, I know that he's into Christmas the way he wanted to be.

At first, I worried Pyro would hate us continuing for the Santa role while he was supposed to get it. But he's searching for his own peace.

And the part of me that still has the draw of love knows it's with a fireball Cupid who needs to see what's right in front of him.

"Can I help with the icing?" Rómán asks, tugging on Arson's shirt. Rómán's skin tone is a dark fuchsia. The perfect mixture of his dad and me. His hair is curly but dark, his little horns are growing in, and he's got the darkest wings sprouting.

Most draegyn don't get their flyable set until they're ten or so. But every single day, he stretches them, hoping to fly sooner rather than later.

"Yes, my little spitfire," Arson answers, lifting Rómán onto the counter. He kisses his forehead and continues to knead the dough.

Rómán pokes at it, licking his finger while I chuckle. Arson peers at me with love and a spark of desire, and I just know he's going to want a third baby.

We've talked about it a lot. Especially since Ash turned one two weeks ago. His eyes burn for me in a way that keeps me warm, even in the coldest parts of winter.

He licks his lips and then raises an eyebrow. His silent way of asking if I want him. Not that he can't tell. Between my arousal perfuming the air and our bond, he's well aware.

As Ash falls asleep, I lift her and take her to her little bed. She and Rómán sleep in the same room. He likes to watch over his sister. Telling us he's her protector. Their bond is strong and heartwarming. Something I wished me and my siblings had sooner.

Once she's down for her nap, Rómán follows suit. As I'm tucking him in, Arson comes from behind me, his shirtless back pressing heat into me.

"Can't wait anymore," he rasps hungrily.

I'll be honest, having kids makes our sex life a lot harder. We do send the kids to Pyro and my sisters often.

Hades, even my parents take them. They were angry at first that I sought out love. But then they saw us together.

Out of all things, they knew love.

Arson leads me from our kids' room and all the way into the spare room at the other side of our new cottage. It's far enough that I can be loud and won't wake our kids.

He lifts me when we're halfway there, his mouth meeting mine. "I want another one." It's so attractive when he's like this. The fact that he loves our children is beautiful and I fall for him a little more each time I see him with them.

"Me too," I admit, wanting another as well. I think I want two. "Is there a way to have twins?" He chuckles, his eyes gleaming with mischief.

"Not sure, but I can fuck you twice as much and see if that doubles the odds," he promises against my throat.

"Think you'll go into another melt soon?"

Crazy enough, every time we've gotten pregnant has been during a melt. And as much as we're busy with Christmas, I want it now.

"Not sure," he responds. "But my parents mentioned there's a way to induce one when you want to breed, and fuck, baby, I do want to breed you."

My eyes widen as I think of having a self-induced sex-fest, and I squirm, thinking of the constant pleasure. "We'll need to send them to one of our siblings."

"Pyro or Val will be fine," Arson states. "Your sisters sent a letter, they're causing mayhem in the human realm. Somewhere in a place called Cancun?"

I chuckle, thinking of that place they always get lost in. My sisters are wild. If they find love one day, I have no doubt it'll be with the same man and a fight will commence.

"Enough about them, let's practice some baby making," I say, wanting to escape reality for a little bit.

As soon as we're in the room, he tosses me on the bed. In the bedside drawer, he pulls out the candy cane dildo, an exact replica of his cock. His eyes heat as he goes into the closet to grab the sex swing he made me for Valentine's Day last year.

It's my newest favorite way for him to be inside me.

He latches it on to our ceiling, his eyes glowing. "Not sure if we have time but I'm going to strap you up and fuck you anyway."

"Hurry," I whisper, loving when he puts me up there.

He locks our room door, turning on the mic for the kids' room. I stand, naked, bending at the waist so he can lock me in. The straps go around my thighs and I use the bed to hold myself up.

He lubes up my ass, stretching me with his fingers before he inserts the candy cane. "Fuck, you're phenomenal, all filled up with me."

Reaching between my thighs, he feels the wetness sliding down. His tongue licks at it, sucking my clit while I wiggle. It's no use, he has me bound entirely, unable to move an inch.

He eats me out while pumping the candy cane in and out of me. Then when I shake from head to toe, he enters me with two fingers, pressing on my g-spot. His mouth latches onto my clit and I explode for him.

As I'm still moaning out my release, he's standing behind me. "I love feeling my cock against your toy. It's like I'm filling you up twice."

"Please, fill me. I want to taste it."

"Dirty fucking girl," he growls, pumping into both holes. I cry out as he makes sure to change his angle. Each thrust bringing stars behind my eyes. I'm so close to coming again, my release from earlier still leaking down my thighs.

Reaching between my legs, he brushes over my clit. "You're making such a mess, wasting that cum, how am I supposed to eat it when you're giving it to the bedsheets, hmm? Don't you want to feed it to me?"

I frantically nod but it's no use, I'm seeing stars as he fucks me in both holes. Screaming louder than I should, he rams into me, growling his release. His cum sprays and he pulls out, painting my ass. The little pumps are felt across my cheeks.

He rubs them over, drawing little shapes. Then he's leaning forward, licking me. "You're so good to me, mate. Taking my cum." When I only whine in response, he lets out a deep chuckle. "Want a taste?"

"Please."

He slaps my ass and then sinks inside my pussy for his cum. Coming to the other side of the bed, he pushes his wet fingers into my mouth.

"Mrs. Claus loves my cum in her mouth, doesn't she? Drinks it all up and always begs for more." He digs inside me for more cum, putting it in my mouth again. "So greedy for my cock and the sweetness it gives."

I nod, sticking out my tongue. He knows what I want. Standing, he places his still stiff candy cane dick on my tongue, rubbing all over it. He shoves down my throat, choking me immediately. I cry out across his length as he thrusts faster and harder.

Drool leaks from my lips and he smiles. "Cock hungry, my wife." He continues his pace and then grips my hair, using it for leverage. "Get ready for my cum. Don't swallow it."

It's a demand I hate to listen to, but then he's pulsing in my mouth, his peppermint flavor coating me. I swallow a little, so as not to choke, and fuck do I want to drink it all.

When he pulls out, he falls to his knees. His eyes burn with desire, he's so aroused and feral for me.

Tentatively, he traces my bottom lip with his thumb. The traces of his cum drips and he reaches forward to lick it clean. Then he's pressing his tongue into my mouth, stealing his own release.

Our tongues swirl with it and we share the taste. He groans and I cry out as his fingers find my sensitive clit. He doesn't stop kissing me until I'm writhing with my final orgasm.

"Merry Christmas, Joyful. And a happy fucking..." he trails of, kissing the scar from the mating mark. "New year."

# THE END

# KEEP READING FOR THE FIRST THREE CHAPTERS OF INCUBUS DESTINIES

# PROLOGUE

**W**ar comes in all shades of blood. The eight kingdoms fighting for supreme rule taught me that. Honor thy people, die by thine honor.

Since I could hold a sword, one has been sheathed to my back. Heavy, long, and unceremonious, Viantra Laitheborn, commander in arms.

I'm supposed to be the leader who saves and conquers. Today was brutal and swift, but a winning match nonetheless:

Until they came... the *marbhsídhe*. *Dead fae*. Overtaking and undermining any progress Caithdor made in the last few months.

We were reaching the Anord borders, succeeding in our fight for our territory. We were *so close*.

Pain lingers in my chest. Not from the gaping wound my cuirass didn't entirely protect from happening, but the soul-deep kind from losing so many people I've loved since creation.

Metal clinks loudly. The snicks of swords hitting one another melt in the background of the screams of people slowly dying around me.

The slice of arrows whirring in the air warns me of what's to come. We're losing. The Warwick Infantry has failed.

I'm weakened. Faefolk surround me, weapons drawn, and I swing in time to avoid another jab. Then, parrying the next massive hit sent my way, I turn just in time to see another coming behind me. Heaviness fills my chest and arms, my heart beating slower with these thoughts.

My body's tired, worn, and needs to rest. I never thought my end would come from exhaustion, but that time is here.

I've realized where my legacy will finish on a battlefield with the dead trees on the moor of the Chaos Kingdom. They're winning. The Anord king will become the king of kings, and we'll lose more than we bargained for. At least I won't need to see it, as my end has come, and Cryptia can take me back home.

As if time slows, the black steel of the fae's sword comes toward me. I don't keep my eyes open, wanting my fate to be left to Cryptia. The last thought to be of the shores of Caithdor, surrounded by zuju fruit, meinshine, and sea glass. *Peace.*

A loud ring of steel hitting steel forces my gaze open, my eyes landing on whom could only be described as war personified.

Sweat, oil, and grime cover his angelic face. His lavender skin is hit perfectly by the falling suns, stunning me. But, awe, that's where I'm stuck.

Long, deep amethyst hair whips in the air, unruly, as he swiftly attacks my assailant. Tendrils of darkness fan his face, like death come to bring them all to their knees. He's beautiful. Unreal. Is he my guide to the afterlife?

His eyes don't meet mine, but fire resides there as he disarms each *marbhsídhe* charging us both. Only kings were bestowed with the fates-of-fire in their gaze. It gave them power, much like my king, Aegan. This hulking creature reflects a bright purple, a promise of pain worse than death.

In the minutes I watch the unfolding of his wrath, something inside me blazes. A burn, and if it were lower—where the blade struck me earlier—I'd have believed it to be from that wound. But as I kneel, feeling all air stolen from my lungs, I know this man is the cause.

My soul knows.

It yearns.

My soul bound.

*Mine.*

# CHAPTER ONE

## VIANTRA

We exist for a reason. And once we die, we discover why... isn't that the saying?

I've lived my life in a box. Square, confined, not truly living. Maybe that's why going back home felt like a new adventure, a place to explore and find anew. Damnation is never simple, and the lost part of me, trying to find its home, really should've foreshadowed that.

I shouldn't have returned with Drew, but my loyalty to Aegan and fear for my best friend's safety overpowered the reality of seeing Alios again. Then there's that part of my soul forever bound to him that probably propelled me too.

Now, they were both safe. The only cost was my betrothal to the man who broke every piece of me, collecting them all like sea glass for his own tortured keeping.

I left Darchon—my beloved realm—for a reason. That reason stands before me now. His eyes tear me limb from limb, narrowed and roaming, while also dissecting each pulled-apart piece of me as he stays on specific body parts on his venture. I'm a mere inspection beneath his cruel stare.

What led us to the moment of angst and discomfort, palpable and uncertain?

He's so beautiful and vicious, twined together like the vesper spurs from home. The roots dug deep, braided beneath the grounds, historical, unending.

Shuffling from foot to foot, my stiffness doesn't falter. My body is wound tight, each second passing as it reinforces its stronghold. I'm protecting myself, shielding him from doing me more harm.

"I shouldn't have come back," I assert, placing my hands behind my back. Ever the soldier. It's a statement. Very bold, especially standing before the King of Collithe. The one who kills without remorse, anyone who defies or disrespects.

"No, no, you shouldn't have," he exudes, finally filling the silence. The breadth of his spread arms is almost a challenge for me to step forward, come closer, and give in to the bond we shared long ago.

It's barely there now, a frail weathering rope, the little pieces dangling like they're staying out of spite and not out of resilience.

"I'll leave then," I shrug. Part of me refutes that, keeping me stuck on this rocky ground. A rock and a hard place, no? That's where I've been for so long. That's where this bond has gotten me, wedged—unable to truly escape and detach.

He steps closer, his body so massive and hulking. It should scare me how much bigger he is than I am. It's the fairy blood. We're much smaller than fae—especially in comparison to incubi men.

My body rumbles, heat overwhelming every single part of my skin as he radiates a type of sensation that brings me closer. I've taken an involuntary step now, our bodies far too close for comfort.

"But you won't, wife. Will you? Because you're mine now. You've vowed yourself to me."

I close my eyes at the mere acknowledgment. In the eyes of Cryptia, the creator of all, we may not have completed our bond, but we are bound in every other way.

"I'm not your wife," I argue.

"Yet," he parries, his eyes glinting. "In three weeks, you'll be mine for good."

It's the deal I struck—time. Three weeks and Alios would allow me to get used to being the queen of his people. They think we're already bound and are just waiting for the proper time for an authentic ceremony. He needs me, and to keep them safe, I need him.

His body overwhelms me as he chips away more space between us. My feet are stuck in this prison of uncertainty and need.

I've been starved for nearly a millennium; morsels were my only offering in the human world.

*Untouched.*

Not his.

Yet his all the same.

They were humans. Unworthy. Not my soul bound.

"I will," I grit out, wanting to hold some type of ignorance, a small ounce of hatred. Something I've kept close to survive, to avoid the truth beneath the emotions.

The fact that we're eternal. And no matter how much I hate him, our destinies are intertwined in the stars, the suns, and all three of our moons.

His hand reaches out, not touching me, but it radiates the kind of buzzing that only a soul bound could ever offer. I'm desperate for him to close the distance, steal away the empty feeling inside my chest.

It's lonely, barren of true fulfillment.

"So close, *Sith*," he whispers, his voice hoarse, like he's barely hanging onto the thread we both pretend isn't nearly gone. Distance between soul bound slowly killed one another. We're lucky to be alive.

His fingers slowly move like they're reaching for something. Trying with all their might to connect with my skin without physically seeking me out.

I can't let Alios touch me. I can't get too close, or I'll crumble to his wants and needs. I need to be steadfast and strong and do what is necessary so Drew and Aegan can be together and happy.

They deserve that.

Closing my eyes once more, I inhale shakily, my palms sweating with every exhale. "I must go. I'm needed elsewhere," I lie. In a way, it's not untrue. I've been gone so long that I'm sure my attention is required somewhere. Before leaving, I had a role. Things I did to help the Caithdorians. My kin.

Caithdor—*the Warwick Kingdom*—is the most beloved home of incubi and succubi. While Collithe—*the Starless Kingdom*—is dark and deep with forest greens and glowing luminescence to make up for the lack of stars in their territory. We're under the same sky, yet somehow, theirs doesn't have the stars above to guide them. Caithdor is vibrant magentas and baby blues, the most chartreuse of greens, and mountains tall and wide. It's home, even if I've forgotten the scent of vespers and loliath when spring colors the valley.

It's the home both Aegan and I were ripped from. So what has come of it now? The alliance between Caithdor and Collithe ended when Alios picked power over allegiance, setting a new war between people. Aegan losing his kingdom wasn't something he ever recovered from. Now that he's back, making amends may not be viable.

So much has had to have changed in my time away from home.

Going to Dalphenia took most responsibilities away. Sure, I helped other fae assimilate to the culture, even if we should've had better options, but I never stayed the warrior I was always raised to be.

I was a protector of the lands, a general in the Warwick Infantry. Fighting in the war of eight kings was my legacy. Losing that has left me feeling empty for so long.

When the wars hadn't begun, I was simply a soldier in another form. Hunting, watching, and ensuring our borders were safe from monsters and fae alike. My duty was to my clan, the faelings, and my family's legacy.

Alios breaks through my thoughts as his face tilts. Almost in amusement and knowledge. He was the king, after all. He knows what I'm needed for and what I'm not.

Being gone means so many things that are unknown to me now. What are my rules, and where do I go from here?

"You're Collithe's queen, Viantra. You're no longer infantry," he explains, a bit of pride hinting at the mention of my new place here. His eyes narrow before his hand slowly falls from the space it had settled between the stagnant air and my face.

"I'm not the queen, Alios. I'm the puppet," I rebut. "Merely a tool for your enormous ego." His jaw tics and his eyes darken, causing the violent glint of amethyst I've only seen him show his enemies to glow vibrantly.

"You're my queen, *Sith. My* soul bound."

"Words," I hiss, my eyes glowing as hatred winds around my barb-wired heart. "They're words and not actions. Actions were your betrayal and my choice to leave here. Of course, I'll do what I must to save my friends, but this—" I wave between us harshly. "—is merely words shared between an incubi and succubi forced together."

"This is destiny," he declares, eating up the sparse distance between us. Our noses are almost touching, his breath mingling with my own.

His scent wafts between us. But, gods, my knees wobble as the sweet nectar of our bond consumes my senses. My chest rapidly moves in a succession of my heartbeats, then slows as if it naturally knows what to do.

No.

Not *this*.

I've never been taken by a man, never allowed anyone inside me. My body knows, and if the pheromones rising from Alios offers anything, it's signaling that information to him too.

"Viantra," he rasps, his voice trailing across my lips. My weakened sex energy tendrils don't fight, and it's hard enough for me to keep them back.

"I must go."

Reluctantly, I take a step back, then another. My feet fight me for every movement away from my mate. His eyes flame; the promises there are too much for me to accept.

"You can't run forever, my wife."

*I will do what I can,* I promise to the open air.

## CHAPTER TWO

### ALIOS

"You thought forcing her to mate with you would be the best option?" Aegan scoffs. Since he arrived, he's been a pain in my ass. Not much has changed during his time away. He's still arrogant to me and charismatic to our people. Yet, he comes to my part of the castle every day just to listen to me complain.

Like old times.

"What was I to do? She's mine," I grumble, thinking of how her dark hair trailed across her back, her eyes a vibrant white as anger hit them.

She was breathtaking to witness, and I knew I could do that forever if she allowed me to.

Aegan shakes his head, his lips titling as he holds back a laugh. "If I've learned anything about Viantra over the years, it's that she doesn't like being told what to do unless there are swords, blood, and death involved."

My mind races back to the moment of the wars, when she nearly died at my feet. The moment she recognized something my mind wouldn't allow.

Something propelled me to her, the fierce warrior fighting off eight different faefolk. Her knees grew weak, and she fell to the ground. Yet still, she fought them off, swinging as they attacked, even under the weight of her exhaustion.

I watched from my higher view, having just killed several of my own assailants. But, when the look over her eyes passed and she went from conqueror to the martyr of acceptance, I couldn't stand back.

Jumping from my vantage point, I rushed to her. Slicing every being that so much as breathed in her direction. At the time, I just didn't know it was our bond that brought me there. She was my mate, a warrior way beneath my age and station, and I did everything to avoid that acknowledgment.

"How do I earn her forgiveness?" I question aloud. Aegan somehow got his mate, she didn't fight their bond, but Viantra hates me.

Aegan goes to the meinshine vault, where it had always been, and grabs a zuju-enhanced one. The vibrant blue glowed in the dimly lit room, reminding me how vastly different colors had become since Viantra arrived.

For so long, everything dulled, each moment less than the last.

"Earning her forgiveness isn't and shouldn't be the goal," he explains. But isn't that what she wants? Me to beg and crawl at her feet?

Aegan pours a tumbler, handing one to me soon after. "The goal is earning her trust, and if she chooses to forgive you, that's her choice." He takes a gulp of his glowing drink, his eyes closing as he swallows. "I've forgotten how nice food is at home."

"Is the human realm not what the other kings made it out to be?"

They've always boasted on how wondrous it was, visiting a place of new realities. He shakes his head, his eyes still withdrawn, focusing on his drink. "For a visit, I'm sure it feels like a wicked getaway. Something tantalizing and untouchable. But it becomes overwhelming when you're forced into a world with technology and cultures that don't make sense."

I forced him away due to jealousy and rage. After the war, Viantra came to Collithe every chance she could, but she was too young. Life had not been lived before then.

Her crush seemed irrational.

That is until she started bringing Aegan—her king, my enemy. There are reasons Collithe and Caithdor were separated many years before. Her getting him to my home put me on edge, and while I hadn't accepted it yet, that wasn't why.

My mouth touches the glass tentatively, recognizing what I'd taken from them both weighing heavily on me.

"I was jealous of you," I admit. My eyes roam over his now attentive gaze. Surprise meets me. Wide eyes and an open mouth would be much more comical if not for the mood.

"Thought I'd never see the day," he mocks, a wrinkle in his brow deepening. "You ruined so much." He pours another glass, shaking his head. "If not for my Drew, I'd hate you still."

A part of me understands this. Aegan lost his kingdom and throne. In exchange, I lost Viantra.

"Was she... happy?" I grit, not wanting to know if she found comfort in others. He all but admitted her innocence previously, but that doesn't mean love hasn't existed.

I wander to the massive windows lit by the glowing trees and candles surrounding us. If Aegan notices my hesitance, my need to know things without genuinely wanting to, he doesn't mention it.

"I feel as if joy came and went," he admits, standing next to me. Our shoulders bump as if we didn't grow to hate each other over the years. "She had moments where hope lived in her, but the light—her true happiness—never quite met her eyes."

The bitter part of me is glad since I never found peace. She stole it, eradicating it from my personal dictionary when she chose Aegan over me. However, the piece she strangles from my heart saddens with the knowledge she's been hurting too.

She was alone *too*.

"She missed you."

I turn to him. Anger still festered inside my rib cage like a beast ready to rip free. "Yet, she left with you."

"She didn't think it would be permanent," he argues. "Viantra will never admit it, but she tried going back. There were tragic moments. Things she'd hate for me to tell you. The desperation she clung to for years slowly died out. Until she found Drew, she was less alive."

Emotion grips me, holding my breath hostage. She wanted me. Even if the world severed our tie.

"Can she still hear your thoughts?" I rasp, wanting to dislodge his organs for their shared connection, and I can't.

He immediately shakes his head, taking another gulp as he gathers his words. I wish I had that patience. To absorb information as it comes, recognize the negative and positive before spouting off. It's something I've still never maturely handled. If anything, my impatience and cruelty have grown since she left.

My people fear me. For that, they're silently trying to remove me from my throne.

"When I finished my bond with Drew, I lost my connection to Viantra and the rest of the camp in Dalphenia. It's peaceful, only being in control of my own emotions and thoughts. It took a lot of restraint to avoid the others on Earth."

"Was it harder there?" Curiosity piques my interest.

"Yes, humans didn't sustain me. Drew being with me was the first time I felt complete." He runs a hand through his hair, his eyes wild with love. "I've felt insatiable for so long." His admission throws me off. I've been starved for a thousand years, but the way he talks is how I've felt my entire life. Incomplete, always hungering for more.

Part of me wonders if that's where my need for power thrives, the need to fulfill the emptiness deep inside me.

We seem to drift in silence, his eyes wandering to the door repeatedly. Similar to my pull to Viantra, his to Drew appears to keep him busy.

At least his mate desires him, not just the craving to make him bleed out.

# CHAPTER THREE

## VIANTRA

"You're a lot quieter here," Drew mentions, noting my absence as we sit at the fountain of fortune. Its statuesque features haunt me. It's the last place I visited before Alios broke me.

"This place harbors a lot of pain," I admit, touching the smooth white material. I mean, in general. Darchon, or more specifically, Collithe, harbors a lot of pain. Our feet dangle into the waters. This statue of Cryptia, her arms reaching above, the fear in her eyes, it's haunted me for ages. We're raised, told that this fountain portrays your guide.

Mine led me to the baths, where my mate fucked another.

I close my eyes, hurt robbing me of all peace.

A tentative touch on my shoulder brings me face-to-face with Drew. She's almost golden now, gold-touched and brimming with light. Jealousy clogs my lungs as I attempt not to be bitter.

"It's okay that you're hurting." Her words are kind, her hands offering me a semblance of calm as she pats me as a sister would. "Have you considered talking to Alios about it?"

Immediately, I shake my head. He's the last person who gets to offer kindness and see my pain. "What could he do but cause me more distress?"

"Understand you," she responds immediately. "No one understands a mate's pain more than your mate."

He doesn't seem to be aching like me, desperate for a touch, a taste, anything other than a power trip.

I stand, my feet planted on the marble floor as little fish swim around me. Then, moving toward Cryptia, I swear she moves to eye me. My hands reach for hers, needing to know if I'd get another outcome other than the one before. Guide me, Goddess.

*"You must only touch her hands," Mother Mithia explains to Saryah and me. We peer at one another, our eyes meeting with hope. We're children, faelings who lost their families to wars or abandonment. Mithia is our caretaker, someone who teaches, loves, and trains us for battle.*

*"Once you touch her hands, you receive your gift if you're one of the many royal Darchon bloodlines. Then, you'll be destined by her touch when you're older."*

When one is a faeling, we don't know our origins in most cases. When we touch the statue, we learn if we're more than just faelings—if we have a purpose. When I first felt Cryptia's hands, I was given the gift of illusions, shifting what someone sees to what I create. It helped a lot in the wars over the years, allowing me to hide or disguise, helping those in need. Many didn't have powers; many were just faelings.

Alios, Aegan, and the six other kings were created specially. Their bloodlines and their predecessors gave gifts unique to each territory. Alios can convince the entire region he's a good man. His touch isn't needed to have power over others. Whereas Aegan's touch was necessary to do the same.

As my hands hover over the statue that gave me the destiny of pain, part of me pauses with fear.

"What will happen this time?" Drew breaks my bubble of anxiety with her soft voice. I turn to her, her eyes glowing as if they're craving Aegan. Something I've recently learned is a trait of their bond. Jealousy lingers inside me for their connection, the comfort, the needs they meet for each other, and the constant love they both show.

"I don't know," I admit, tipping my head down to avoid her gaze. "Cryptia never gives any warning, she only decides your fate. Sometimes, she doesn't even tell you with motivations or nudges. Instead, it's given to you randomly."

Drew stands, walking over to me. The water swishes, her body next to mine. Grabbing my wrist, she rubs a circle along my veins—a comfort thing humans seem to do. "No matter what happens, I'm here, always. Aegan too."

A burning sensation hits the backs of my eyes as her words dig deep. For so long, I've felt like a faeling, someone whose only purpose was war. Even when in Dalphenia, I've felt like a protector and provider, never worthy of love and adoration.

Offering a silent nod, I allow her to press my hand down on Cryptia's hands, feeling the smooth stone offer coldness and insight.

My eyes close of their own accord as memories swiftly hit me.

*My finger lingers on the paper that Dagmar brought. Her little claw held on to my finger as I untied the little string holding it to her. Dagmar is a royal carrier, a gala, the only bird species trusted enough to communicate between royals.*

*You're in Collithe again, aren't you, deirfiúr?*

*The message came from Aegan. My king, and basically my brother. After the war of eight kings, he took me in, allowing me to roam the realm freely. I was the first faeling to be given such a gift.*

*I've been sneaking over to Collithe at every chance to be able to see him... my mate. Alios. He's training. His feet are planted on the ground as he spars with another guard.* His hair is down, unruly, and I catch myself wanting to run my fingers through it.

His lips tilt as he bests his opponent, his eyes lighting with pride. Swiping his leg under the other man's, Alios trips him. The sword Alios wields bears down, hitting the man on the ground in his chest. While the blades are genuine, the man wears a cuirass, protecting his chest.

Absently, I rub my fingers across mine, where my scar hides beneath my glimmer, not to be seen again.

Alios places his sword in his hilt and saunters away, his ego fed from the win against one of his best trained. I couldn't resist following behind Alios, my heart picking up speed as he weaved through the trees to the bathing pit in the center of Collithe.

It's beautiful. Foliage surrounds, and as the suns are setting, the bioluminescence is present. That's something that's always drawn me to this territory. It feels like home, a place where you escape into the darkness, and only the glow can guide you.

As I tiptoe toward the water area, he begins undressing. It's unbecoming of me to look at him as he removes his clothing, but I can't look away.

I've been watching him for the last few years, enjoying how he controls every movement with grace.

He never sees me, but I know deep inside that he's my soul bound. One day, he'll see it too. A twig snaps as my legs carry me nearer, and he's immediately facing me, bare-chested and glistening with exertion.

His eyes glow dangerously amethyst, like a firefly in the night, waiting to catch its prey. "I don't like being followed, child," he rasps, his voice old and bothered. He's not a kind man, or so everyone tells me.

Chills break out over me as he walks in my direction, a hum dancing beneath my skin as he grows nearer. "I know you're out here. I've seen you watching me."

His voice carries much farther than the twelve feet expanse between us, but I only quiet my breath and attempt to push down the way my heart pounds.

His low hiss fills my ears when he nears the foliage I'm hiding behind. "You may hide now, using whatever mind trick protecting you, Sith, but you cannot hide forever."

I shake as I'm removed from the memory, thinking of the first time he called me fairy before I even knew what I was. I don't even know where I come from.

Before gathering my groundings, I'm thrown into another.

Alios stands in his chambers, his chest rippling with his muscles, statuesque. His body flexes with every movement as if chiseled from gods and marble, and I watch as a voyeur once more.

"Cryptia," he breathlessly sounds out the word as if he hasn't prayed to her in a long time. "Will she ever forgive me?" His voice breaks at the last word, the sound nearly a whisper, so foreign and soft for such an angry man.

An ache forms in my chest, a tight feeling like something being squeezed. It aches all the way to my toes, forcing me to grip it. The discomfort isn't something describable, but it's as if I'm feeling how Alios is feeling and not entirely my own reaction.

He drops to his knees, the thud hitting my ears as much as the groan that escapes his lips. "I don't deserve her, Goddess. If I wither away, let her find happiness, okay?"

A silent tear befalls my cheek, wetting my skin with glitter and heartache. The tightness hitting me seems to close around the organ in my chest, making sure every piece of that man's pain is something I experience too.

My eyes close of their own volition, needing to rip the agony Alios is in. I'm back with Drew as soon as I do, but she's no longer touching me. Instead, she's being held by Aegan a few feet away, his arms around her as he consoles her.

Did she see it too?

Or did Cryptia feel her presence and prepared her for her own downfall?

He peers at me, and questions sit between his eyebrows.

"I've got to go," I excuse myself, wanting to hide away forever. Unfortunately, things just got a lot more complicated. Is Cryptia asking me to forgive him, guiding me to his side? Or is she simply showing me what's in store for our future?

You can read Incubus Destinies in
Kindle Unlimited, available on Amazon.

# MAEVE BLACK

MONSTERS, FAE, SMUT
& MORE SMUT

## MEET MAEVE

Maeve Black writes fantasy, paranormal, and monster romance that they've always wanted to read. As someone who is queer, fat, and Latine, Maeve tries to be diverse and inclusive with all works, helping others see that the world isn't just a social construct. They love reading, playing fantasy video games, and drawing in their spare time. Maeve wants to be known for their spice and unique takes on the monsters they choose to write.

Printed in Great Britain
by Amazon